PAYDIRT

University of Western Australia Press New Writing Series

The *New Writing* series introduces creative writing from postgraduate writing programs in universities across Australia, which for the last three decades have produced exciting new works from emerging and established writers. The series also publishes the creative writing of Australian academics. By introducing this series, we are recognising the role of Australian universities in nurturing and supporting writers, and contributing to the continuing production of Australian writing.

Series editor Terri-ann White is actively involved in the literary culture of Australia: as a writer, bookseller, publisher, editor and award judge. Her novel *Finding Theodore and Brina* (2001) is studied in university courses in Spain, the United States and Australia. She published a collection of stories, *Night and Day*, in 1994, has edited anthologies and been published widely. She is currently director of UWA Press and of a cross-disciplinary research centre at The University of Western Australia.

Titles in series

Forthcoming

PAYDIRT

Kathleen Mary Fallon

University of Western Australia Press

University of Western Australia Press
Crawley, Western Australia 6009
www.uwapress.uwa.edu.au

Publication of this book was assisted by a
publication grant from the University of Melbourne.

National Library of Australia
Cataloguing-in-Publication entry:

Fallon, Kathleen Mary.
Paydirt.
ISBN 978 1 920694 97 5.
1. Family—Australia—Fiction.
2. Stolen generations (Australia)—Fiction.
3. Aboriginal Australians—Social conditions—
Fiction. 4. Abused children—Australia—
Fiction. I. Title. II. Title : Call me mum
(Motion picture).
A823.4

Cover photographs: by Sue Ford
(in the collection of the artist);
in collaboration with: Diane Bellear
Photograph of the author by
Victoria Rowland

*Consultant editor Susan Midalia
Designed by Becky Chilcott, Chil3, Perth
Typeset in 10 pt Janson by Lasertype
Printed by McPherson's Printing Group*

Dedicated to the memory of Ephraim Bani (1944–2004) and to the Torres Strait Islanders who have spent their lives working for the preservation of Torres Strait Island languages and culture.

PAYDIRT

sought out by
the yellow-white
of my headlights

the earth
void dirt

the old tip truck
full of dirt
lumbering along
the road

weeping-extinct-
animal-totem
last-of-his-tribe
animal totem
mothermary
veil-of-tears

the weight of
the earth
upon itself
forcing out
water

the last (fluid) gasp
of the dead
body
eliminating

the number plate
reads
PAYDIRT

KATE

ALL HER CHICKENS
(English language title)

MERIAM KARA SAGIM
(Meriam Mer — Eastern Islands language title)

NAU KAZIL LAK MANGI LAK MUDTHA
(Kala Lagaw Ya — Western Islands language title)

Good, sit over there then sonny boy. It's a big plane and the further away the better. I'm sick to death of you too you little shit. It's like living with Luna-bloody-Park living with you Wassa Boy but this is the last straw. Dellkeith's right, you've ruined my life … *run run as fast as you can you can't catch me I'm the Gingerbread Man* … God I need a drink after all that. Racist mongrels, speaking to us like that, how bloody dare they. I swear I'll go to Anti-discrim like I said I would, I swear I will. Just look at him, filthy and stinking the place out, I feel sorry for whoever he sits next to, they're in for a bad trip. Where the hell have you been for the last two weeks Wassa? Jesus Christ, look at the state you're in. Who on earth did that chop-job on your poor hair? I can't bear to look at you. And where did you get all the gear? That Primate skateboard stuff costs a fortune. I wanted to buy it for your birthday but it was too xey. I can't bear to think how you got the money.

I'm going to have to call the cops—again—when we land and tell them you've turned up—again. I had to really heavy them to take me seriously this time, they won't even bother taking your details next time you piss off. I should just let you go off and be 'free', piss off to 'tropical paradise with your real mother'. Everyone keeps telling me to cut the apron strings. It's just the excuse the Department needs, the last straw they've been waiting for. They'd whip you away and into that nice warm place in Care at Woodbrook Cottages they've got earmarked for you. Little shit. I should just let nature take its course, see how 'free' you'll be making fucking coathangers at the Woodbrook Sheltered Workshop for the Visually Impaired, that's the exciting, challenging career path they have planned for you Warren, my love. We're stuck in auto-reverse Wassa. Your next TV appearance can be on *This Is Your Life*. We'll watch as you're being dragged backwards, back into Woodbrook—again. A nice, neat little circular narrative, delivering the satisfaction of closure.

'Excuse me, stewardess, can I have a whisky, please? Neat. No ice. No soda. Thanks.'

Two and a half hours till I'm face to face with Dellkeith again after all these years. Four and a half till I'm face to face with Flo. God what am I going to say to her? '... Flo ... Mum ...' No, I can't call her that '... Flo ...' There was nothing in the *June Dally-Watkins' Book of Etiquette* Dellkeith gave me for my sixteenth birthday telling me the dot-point protocols for meeting and greeting your Black foster son's Black birth mother. I'm scared shitless. I even rang Link-up. They said they didn't have the resources to deal with **white** foster parents and it was outside their 'brief'. Yeah right! Thanks a lot. I couldn't work out whether it was because I was white or because he was an Islander, wrong kind of Blackfella, that they wouldn't talk to me. Where the hell did he get all that gear? I'm just out of my mind with him. He thinks I'm just nagging. He doesn't understand the seriousness of the situation at all. If the Department finds out what he's been up to it really will be curtains. *To be Section Nined for his own good and that of the community at large*, they wrote. And what if the cops join the dots and dob to them? His only hope now is that his family, his mother, Flo, Flo might be able to talk some sense into him. If

3

only he **could** go back with them but he's got to wait. I'll have to explain it to her even though she's so sick. If he waits a couple of months, just till after he's turned eighteen and out of the control of the Department he can do what he bloody well likes, go where he bloody well likes, and good riddance. He really will be free. It's what we've been after all these years, and now, just when it looks like we're in the clear, the social worker's visits, the surveillance, the control escalates. They still won't change the psychological assessment—*blind and profoundly retarded.* Anyone can see it's nonsense but not them. I think they're being wilfully obtuse. All the work over thirteen years to bring him up 'normal', prove he was 'normal', intelligent, capable, teaching him myself, getting him into decent schools even if it meant changing States or moving across town, sending him to YMCA camp. I can't believe this is happening—again. But I can't tell Flo—'Mum'—Flo how serious it is, she's so sick and so happy that he's well and that. But I'll have to tell her something. He's got to calm down and stop running away and whatever else he's getting up to. He just can't go off like that, even with them, with his family. Not yet. Meeting her again after all these years, she'll calm him down. She's just got to.

What can I say to her? '… good morning Flo … Mrs … um … Mum …' I don't even know what to call her. She says to call her 'Mum' and she calls me 'Mum'. She called me 'Mum' on the phone too. Is she having a go at me? Islander humour? She said, 'You're my son's Mum so we'll call you Mum.' I asked Link-up but they wouldn't or couldn't explain it. Lifeline was more bloody help, at least they listened to me.

'… good evening 'Mum' … ' No, I can't. '… good evening Flo … you're looking well … nice weather … love your colourful Islander frock … oh and here's your son who I've been keeping warm for the last thirteen years … see what a good job I've done … looks better than when you last saw him doesn't he?' …

Listen to that. Dellkeith's daughter alright. The whiteness rising in me. Jesus! All these years with Warren and I can only bring myself to talk to his mother like that. Listen to that stiff-backed, pursed-lipped soul of mine, so nice and white and bright and violent. Will nothing kill that bitter spirit in me? I've got the same face as those gruesome old photos on the walls at home in *Dellkeith*. All perked up with this mad pride to hide this even madder shame. 'Your forebears', as Dellkeith so proudly points out. All that popcorn pink scabbing the map of world empire, it's the cloth I'm cut from … *run run as fast as you can you* … Great-grandma, who was virtually bought by a man on the docks as she stepped off the ship in Bundaberg or Rockhampton, one of those godforsaken holes. She was sixteen, alone and pregnant to 'the local priest back home in England.' Sure! It was always *the local priest*. And all the rest lies too, just silence and lies and what I try to read in their hard, ugly, ruined faces. Same as mine in any mirror.

'… hello Flo … so you just let the Department take your sick baby and that was that …' A voice like a balled fist. The Protector's wife will be serving afternoon tea on the lawn. You wouldn't dare touch a white woman.

'… what happened on Thursday Island fifteen years ago Flo? …Warren was in such a bad way when he came down south … how did he get that bad?' … But what use will digging up all that past do us? No! Let sleeping dogs lie, as Dellkeith would say. No! I've got to stop all this and just focus on him and the immediate danger, that he's got to stay out of the Department's clutches until he turns eighteen. We'll deal with all the rest later. The last time she saw him he was three and so sick and fucked up. Maybe she'll tell me what really happened one day. Not now though. And she's so sick. How will he cope if she dies? It might make it worse. Of course it'll make it worse you fuckwit. I don't know if I'm doing the right thing and there's no one to ask, no one, only Lifeline. I'm a regular caller there now or, as they call me, a 'stuck' caller. They'll only give me ten minutes each call because I'm not in crisis yet. They gave me a crisis phone number for when we're in Brisbane though.

That phone call out of the blue like that last week. No name, just some Islander woman asking for Warren. I didn't know what to say but thank god I had the presence of mind to get a few details. But who the hell was she and how did she get our number?

As soon as he spoke to Flo and the family on the phone that first time he just took off—again. Without his insulin—again. I've driven the streets night after night looking for him. Been to the hospital casualty departments so many times. Been to the morgue twice. Whenever I heard that a dead Black kid had been brought in. One of them was found in a derelict building with a Hungry Max bag full of glue stapled to his face. Apparently The Bags Are Better at Hungry Max. I've learnt how to mainline Vegemite—cut a flap of skin, spread the Vegie and bandage it up—yeast hit straight into the blood stream. Every time the phone rings I've thought—*diabetic coma* or *Black Death in Custody*. I just keep drinking. It's the only thing that stops the panic. I just don't know where to turn or what to do or who to ask.

Yes I do. The stewardess. What I need's another whisky.

Know where I finally found him last night? Ensconced in this derelict old mansion full of handicapped and psychiatric people. All these poor people just shuffling around on the cement in the backyard waiting for their baked beans on toast for tea. I found him in one of the tiny rooms with a blind and psychiatric couple he said he'd met on the train. The three of them were sitting on this single-mattress bed watching TV, my TV. My TV and video were stolen last week. There was a mountain of unopened jumbo crisp and Twistie packets on one side of the bed and a mountain of empty packets on the other and crates of full and empty bottles of Crystal soft drink stacked against the wall. There were filthy and stinking clothes all over the floor and some supperating in a bucket. I recognised some of his missing shirts amongst the mess. I was so mad I told the creepy Manager that I was going to report the theft to the cops. When I got back with the cops the Owner was there. He got out of his gold Alpha wearing an Armani suit and covered in gold jewellery. He said Warren owed him $500 for breaking a window when he put his head through it trying to fix a blind. The couple swore to the cops that the TV and video belonged to them and the Owner and Manager backed them up. The cops believed them and said I'd have to produce the sales docket. I drove home and got it. That's when one of the neighbours told me she'd seen Warren get out of a gold Alpha, go into the flat and carry out the TV and video. When I returned with the sales docket the couple blubbered and acted totally psycho. The cop was flabbergasted. He said, 'Lady, without that docket I'd never have believed you.' I said, 'They're bunging on this psycho-retard act. I want the bastards charged. This isn't the first time they've stolen stuff from me.' The cop said, 'Well, you'll have to charge your foster son then because he was the one who carried it out to the car, apparently. They knew what they were doing alright. You charge them and you'll look like a real Fagin in the end.'

A couple of weeks ago I got home and the cops were all over the house. This same dumb couple had been to a Magistrate and reckoned Warren and I stole all these things from them. The list read—one cricket ball (old), 4 CDs (Country and Western), 1 pair of diving goggles, 2 shirts (one red, one green), 2 VCRs (sport) etc etc. The cops had threatened Warren and he was crying hysterically. All my clothes and underwear and well, everything, was lying on the floor. 'You always reckon you can fix things, fix this then Little Miss Fix-it!' Warren yelled at me. The fucking cops assumed we were a couple and kept making sexual innuendoes. 'Mrs Warren I presume,' they smirked. The same thing happened just now coming through Security at the airport. Because I had to help him through the metal detector with all his stuff, the idiot Security Guards kept calling me his 'girlfriend' and looking at me like I was filth. Racist, sexist turds. I'm going to go to Anti-discrim I fucking well am.

Stop it! Stop it! He's here now and he's OK. Don't think of all that now. This is urgent. You'll be meeting Flo later and you've got Dellkeith's welcoming arms to pull you back into the bosom of the family. I **think** I'm glad I finally decided to write to them after all this time. It was hard to ask if we could stay there but, apart from anything else, I spent all the money I had on the plane tickets. I can always ring Lucille and borrow some money if things go awry at *Dellkeith*. And the thought of dealing with all this alone in a cheap motel—I really do think they've changed though, gotten older and a bit mellow. I felt so bad that they had to track me down through that TV station after they'd seen Warren on that bloody program. What on earth must they think after seeing that? And having to send a letter via the TV station to their own daughter—they said they'd be happy for us to stay there. 'Let woebegones be bygones,' they wrote. 'Come home to us darling. We are waiting. *Dellkeith* is waiting. ... *run run as fast as you can you can't catch me I'm* ... Oh god! What am I going to do? Relax! Breathe! Think positive, practical thoughts! See Warren and me standing in a bubble of golden light! Get another whisky! Yes!

'... Flo ... 'Mum' ... ' She'll want to know about his life. I've got the happy snaps here. Thank god they don't tell the full story. How can I tell her any of the true story? I wish I could forget. No! I don't want to forget anything. He's taught me everything I know. I want to tell somebody who'll listen; some day I want to try to tell somebody who'll listen, just sit quietly and calmly and tell someone who'll sit quietly and calmly and listen, tell someone the blank, simple, raw facts. Every time I try I get too emotional, too angry, too upset and people think I'm exaggerating. I'm so freaked out I just go on and on and they think I'm crazy. 'You're so theatrical,' my friends say. 'What a drama queen.' Some of them think I got what I deserve, 'Putting all your energy into a male child.' Stupid, dumb, dyke bitches. Think they're sooo radical because they're lesbians. Middle-class twats. I don't see them anymore. A few months ago I was worried because he wouldn't take his Blundies off, even when he went to bed. My friends thought it was a great joke. They smiled smugly and said, 'He's fine. What a character. A real larrikin. A born raconteur. Just cut the apron strings.' The therapist I was seeing at the time got that *concerned look* on her stupid face and said, 'The way you're talking about him sounds just like your own personalised colonialism. He needs to be free, authentic, find his Black heritage. Remember you're white.' I yelled at her, 'I'm white all right, white with fucking anger!' Then she wrote something on the file. One night he collapsed—an infection—'new-moan-u-off-the-bone-in-my-foot', he calls it.

Gangrene's such a laugh. The doctors thought they'd have to amputate. It was touch and go for days. A drunk land-rights lawyer at a party called me 'an assimilationist bitch. You should be ashamed of yourself,' he said. I don't go to parties anymore. One of the social workers at Warren's Big Case Conference last week patted me on the hand and said, 'Have you had your blood pressure checked recently?' Patronising bastard! But who wants to know this stuff? I just have to cop it and shut up. As Dellmay once said when I tried to tell her what was going on, 'Stop! Stop! You dare bring all the filth of the world into *Dellkeith*, the home I've worked so hard to make a haven. Charity begins at home, my girl. That's one thing I do agree with the Black radicals on—like should stick to like.' And Keith said, 'Don't! Don't! I've tried to keep all the sorrow and nastiness of the world out of my life and you kids' lives and now you just go out and bring it all back in. The thing you don't know is that I know all about all of it and I've forced myself to forget and now I don't want to remember. Don't tell me anymore. You'll break my heart again and believe me it was broken long before you were ever even born.' And Dellkeith sang in chorus, 'We aren't going to tell you we told you you'd rue the day. We aren't going to tell you we told you you'd made a rod for your own back. We aren't going to tell you we told you you'd made your own bed and that one day you'd have to lie in it.'

'… Warren screamed all day long when he first arrived at Cherrymead, Flo, just screamed …' Edit! Edit, you stupid bitch! You can't tell Flo that. If anyone even touched him he'd start bellowing, lashing out, punching and kicking and biting like an animal. '… what on god's earth happened to him up there Flo? … the Thursday Island files said *meningitis* … the Brisbane files said *cranial trauma, malnutrition, epilepsy* … recently an ophthalmologist said *iatrogenic disease* ... nice name for a nice big doctor fuck-up with lots and lots of nice wrong drugs, apparently ... I can't make any sense out of any of it ... I've taken him to GPs, neurologists, naturopaths, psychics, podiatrists, psychologists, psychiatrists, reiki masters ... all I know, Flo, is he was fucked over then and he's being fucked over now and I'm still trying to fix the fuck-up and I'm still fucked up myself ... flat line ...' Jesus Christ! I can't talk to her like that.

Matron said, 'Blind and profoundly retarded—meningitis. Never, under any circumstances, is he to be left alone with the other children. A wild man. A wolf boy. The Wild Man of Borneo. Violent and crazy. Brain damaged. There's no hope. Why on earth someone didn't have the mercy to—well—put him out of his misery.' I was nineteen, I didn't know how to—then. Didn't know how to *leave people to their fate*. Didn't realise that some people, routinely, get chucked out with the garbage. Didn't know that it was *professional* to watch them free-falling. Didn't know that it was my job to watch the trained and educated dispensing the benefits of their training and education. Fostering Warren was spitting in their blind eyes; now they're spitting back.

One of the nurses said, 'Imagine what he'll be like when his hormones kick in. No woman will be safe no matter what the dosage.' She was also the one who warned me, after I'd put a red t-shirt on him one morning, 'Never dress a darkie in red. It's a red rag to a bull. They go mad.' As she gave him another handful of stelazine, largactil, meloril, dilantin. She called the three Black kids in the home *Little See-No-Evil, Hear-No-Evil, Speakie-No-Evil*. They were classified as *socially retarded*, in other words *Black*. I can't tell Flo that sort of thing when she's so sick. She seems to think the government did what it said it would, gave him medical treatment and an education, at least that was the gist of our conversation on the phone.

'... he was a wonderful child, Flo ... there are so many stories I can tell you about him ... I can remember the exact day I fell for young Wassa Boy here ... this day I was alone in the playroom and there was an emergency and I had to rush one of the kids out to the dispensary ... I ran back, terrified, because I'd left 'Mad Warren' alone with Moaner ... Moaner was a little girl we had to tie by the wrists to a mattress on the floor because she spent her days moaning and shrieking, trying to bite chunks out of her hands ... as I rushed back I couldn't hear a sound ... I thought, 'My god! He's killed her ...' Edit! I can't tell Flo that. '... and as I got to the room I saw Warren kneeling down beside her ... 'Oh! My god! What's he doing to her?' ...' Edit! You stupid bitch! '... he was holding his hand out and she was smelling it and he was singing that little nonsense song he always sings himself to sleep with ... *a whale car knackie, a whale car knackie* ... he was comforting her, Flo ... none of us had ever even tried ... did you teach him to be like that Flo?

'... and you know Flo, he just got better and better, every day ... eventually he stopped screaming and started to laugh ... one night ... aah! you'll love this one 'Mum', Flo ...' I'll tell her your favourite 'Mr-Smile-On-The-Dial-running-through-the-rainy-night-in-my-wet-nappy-this-is-your-life story' will I Wassa love? '... this one night, after we'd put all the kids to bed, there was a knock on the front door ... it was pissing down outside and cold as hell and we were a bit scared in this big, silent institution ... there were only two of us on night shift ... anyway we open the door and who do you think's standing there in the rain, shivering in his big wet nappy, laughing? ... god love him ... we all did ... big bloody smile on his dial like nobody's business … Mr Smile-on-the-Dial we called him after that … he's climbed out of his cot, Flo … managed to unlock the heavily secured window … climbed down the drainpipe and somehow found his way over two fences and around to the front door … blind and profoundly profoundly something all right.

'… I take him to the Easter Show, Flo … he won't get off the Dodgems … 'Doggie-gems Aunty Katie! Doggie-gems!' … every time another car hits him he laughs … he's laughing so much he can't drive and so more and more cars hit him … he hears me laughing and that sets him off again … he laughs so much he wets himself Flo and we've got to run for the lav … I'd never laughed like that in my life … he taught me joy Flo … I owe him, big time …' I can tell Flo, Mum, that one, she'll love that.

But love, you mixed up those stories on that TV program didn't you? And how on earth did the interviewer get you to say that I locked you up in a chicken coop in the backyard? We never even had a chicken coop. And what on earth's this slop-slop I fed you in a bowl like a dog? And now you're so confused you say it's true because you saw it on TV. I've sat you down a couple of times to remind you about what really happened but you just fly off the handle, go off at me and run away. '… he doesn't like to hear anything sad, Flo, or to be told he's been naughty or done anything wrong, likes to stay upbeat, *keeping up the atmosphere*, he calls it … '

The really scary thing though, is that nowadays Warren only exists when he has an audience, he can't bear to be by himself. 'I made em laugh and I made em cry Katie when I told em me This-is-Your-Life story,' he said when he came home after they filmed that TV program. But he realised what he'd done, months later, at that awful cast-and-crew screening. It was awful. He was so proud, playing Mein Host at the pre-screening drinks, carrying a tray of hors d'oeuvres around, introducing himself as the star of the film. He was sitting beside me in the theatre, excited as hell. I'll never forget it. And, after a while, he leant over to me and whispered, 'They said it was a film Mummy but it's a doctored-mentality isn't it?' And as soon as it was finished he got up and ran out crying and just took off. He was gone for a week that first time, god knows where, the cops couldn't find him, I couldn't find him.

And god only knows what Flo thinks of me after seeing that TV program. I'll have to try to sort that one out.

I wish I could just forget all this. I don't want to forget any of it so I've got to keep forcing myself to remember, or it all slips away, just slips away. My mind's as full of holes as that little social worker, Tiffany's, welfare net.

runrunrun

SHIFTING SANDS
    the social fabric
    a web of lies
    turns to dust
    in my hands
    under my feet
    shifting sands
    nothing to stand on
    no terra firma
    a terra nullius

'... Cherrymead would only keep kids until they turned five, Flo ... and then, if they hadn't been fostered out, they were sent

to Woodbrook, the big State institution on the edge of town
… sometimes Dellkeith would go past it on our Sunday drives
and say, 'That's where you'll end up. Do you know what they do
to naughty children in there?' … us nurses called it the Tip …
I 'Tipped' plenty of kids there on their fifth birthday … none
of us nurses wanted to be the one to do the Tip Run with old
Smile-on-the-Dial, we all knew what he was in for … then he
was guilty of turning five and I was his only hope, I had just
turned twenty-one and was married … now he's guilty of turning eighteen and you're his only hope Flo, you're his biological
mother, he might listen to you.

'… so, his only hope was to be fostered out before he
turned five … one Sunday, hallabloodyloolya … an old couple
… Christians … turned up at Cherrymead to take him out for a
drive … they came back the next Sunday too … so, on the third
Sunday, when the Christians didn't show, I went to Matron and
asked her if they were going to foster Warren … 'No!' she said
… and I can still see her badly permed red head bent over the
Roster … she didn't even look up … 'No!' she said. 'They're
getting a dog instead.' … and I picked up the paperweight and I
smashed it down into her thick skull …' Edit! '… I can still feel
the satisfying thunk …' Fuckin Jesus! Edit you psych bitch! You
did nothing. '… but something hard and cold bunched up inside
me like a balled fist and just said, 'No!—No! No! No! No!' to
all the violence smashing down around him '… all the violence
possible in the world was just crashing down on him Flo … and
it's still crashing down on us … it has never stopped … was it
like that for you too, Flo?'

Anyway, that's when I learnt to fight violence with violence,
when I became the monster you reckon I am today Wassa. It's
true, **I** don't feel anything anymore, but I feel what **you're**

feeling like a phantom limb. I thought, 'Even a fuck-up like me's a better bet than the Tip, Mr Smile-on-Your-Dial.' So I marched in to see the social worker, Tiffany, Tiffy in her pretty little pastel pink ensemble. She said they wouldn't even consider it unless I was married. So I rang Robbie, my poof flatmate, 'Can we talk about this when you get home?' he said. 'No,' I said, 'there isn't time.' We got married the next week, cleaned up the empties, hid the bong, waved goodbye to my Lucille and Robbie's boyfriend, served Tiffany Adora Cream Wafers on matching Shelley Blood and Bone china, filled in the forms and waited.

'Doggie-gems Aunty Katie! Doggie-gems!' he kept yelling as I packed his little suitcase, as I strapped him into his seat belt beside me. 'Doggie-gems Aunty Katie? Doggie-gems?' As I did the Tip Run out to Woodbrook for his Now-That-You're-Five birthday present. Tiffy hadn't processed the paperwork. Thanks Tiff!

And it's true, Blacks regress, revert; Warren was five-and-a-half when he reverted. All the progress he'd made at Cherrymead was lost. They called us Weekend Parents and so Robbie and I would take him out from the Tip every Friday night and take him home for the weekend. He'd often be dressed in filthy shirts that were too small and filthy singlets that were too big and every Friday he'd be worse than the week before. One Friday he'd be in nappies—again; the next he seemed to be deaf; the next he'd be talking baby talk—again. And Tiff still hadn't processed the fucking paperwork. He was drugged out of his mind. One Friday when I picked him up they'd tried to give him a short back and sides and only done half the job. His hair was that thick I suppose they just gave up but he looked awful; they'd shaved half his hair off. That's why I got such a fright to see him today with that haircut, hair sculpture, hair butchery—whatever it is. He looks so bad. It's brought it all back.

Anyway, that Sunday afternoon, when I dropped him back, he ran up the steps and turned and smiled and waved as usual but, when I drove away, I made the mistake of looking in the rear-vision mirror and I saw him crumple to the ground crying as the nurse led him away. Have you ever seen anyone crushed? That's the word, *crushed*. He was crushed. I can't tell Flo any of this. Anyway, I thought, 'I can't keep doing this.'

And then, the next weekend when I rang to say I wouldn't be coming, they said, 'Oh! He's sick anyway.' And when I went out there to see him it took them half an hour to get him ready and he was still filthy, still stank of vomit and piss and shit when they took me into this cement room, just a cell really, and he was lying there on one of those metal gurney things. He was burning up with fever and they reckoned it was a recurrence of meningitis. When he saw me he reached up and took my hand, and this will give you some idea of the type of kid he was, still is, he patted my hand and said, 'Don't worry Aunty Katie, doctor fix.' Shit! He was worried about me, that's what he was like, still is. How could I ever turn my back on a person like that? I've never met anyone else like him. He taught me ridiculous courage, I owe him, big time.

run … run … as fast as … just run … run

THE SINC(E) OF THE PAST—1
    something dead and buried
    in unhallowed ground
    the sinc(e) of the past

just a bundle of hair and teeth
lodged inside her for years
deadpregnant
deadbeat
breach-of-faith birth
the deadblackpapoose
mummymonkey on my back
phantom pregnancy
miscarriages miscarriages miscarriages
not living a life
haemorrhaging a life
someone has fallen into the fit of those shoes
someone has found the shape that waits
someone has fallen through the holes in the welfare net
the tear in the tissue-of-lies social fabric
I'm beside myself
stalked, ghosted, out of focus
just out of arm's reach
in harm's way
the sinc(e) of the past

He nearly died. Sometimes I hoped he would. Hoped something, someone, would *put him out of his misery*. There seemed only a nightmare future for him. He went to hospital. They gave him all these tests—three lumbar punctures; great needles in the spine to take fluid. He just screamed and screamed they hurt so much. For years he screamed if I washed his back. He stopped eating, talking, seeing, hearing, walking, totally incontinent—again. I'd go in and he'd be curled up in that nice, crisp, white hospital bed—trying to die. I'd put my hand up to his face and he'd smell it and make that weird whistling sound of his, and that seemed to comfort him. And I'd sing his little nonsense song to him really softly ... *a whale car knackie, a whale car knackie* ... and that seemed to comfort him.

None of the tests showed anything medically wrong—no sign of meningitis, nothing, and so they sent him back to the Tip. Tiff still hadn't processed the paperwork. I've no idea why it took so long.

I have to keep forcing myself to remember that next Friday night when I went to pick him up. The nurse said, 'Oh! The little crippled boy.' They were already calling him that. And then I saw this creature grunting its way down the dark corridor towards me. It was laboriously pushing itself along on a piece of board with wheels, moaning and grunting and pushing itself along with its hands, straight out of the Middle Ages, like something Goya drew in charcoal. When it got closer I saw it was Warren. He didn't recognise me so I knelt down and held out my hand and he smelt it and started making that weird whistling sound.

I wish I could forget all this. I don't want to forget any of it and unless I keep making myself remember I can feel it just slipping away. If I stop talking I'll disappear; if I stop fighting back I'll die.

While I was packing his bag to take him back to Woodbrook that next Sunday night I knew it was for the last time. I decided I'd have to forget him. I remember saying to Lucille, 'We've got to leave him to his fate now Luce. It's hopeless. I've got to just leave him there to die.' As I was saying it the phone rang and there was a new Tiffany saying that there'd been an outbreak of diphtheria, imagine it, bloody diphtheria, that's what Dellmay's sister May died of back in the twenties, and Woodbrook was in quarantine. 'According to your file,' she said, 'you were wanting to foster Warren on a more permanent basis. Do you still want him?'—like we'd let our lay-by lapse. 'Yes,' I said, and that's how easy it was in the end. I've no idea why the paperwork took so long, and from then on he just stayed home with Lucille and Robbie and me. He still couldn't walk, and he'd cry when he tried, so I used to sit him in the sun and massage his legs with Vicks and tell him the tingling was the warmth of the medicine coming in and fixing them. And we'd take him to the heated baths and he'd swim around and around in his 'Rubber-duckie Aunty Katie. Rubber-duckie'. And soon he was walking as well as ever. 'It's a miracle!' the people cried. You taught me all about miracles, Wassa Boy.

'… we had to detox him, Flo … it took six months before we could finally stop shovelling in the handfuls of stelazine, meloril, largactil, dilantin and I'd send away to Sydney, to a company called Vitaglow I think it was, because it was before health food shops … and they'd send huge tubs of Brewer's yeast, Vitamin A for his eyes, Vitamin C for healing and colds, Vitamin E for scarring, Zinc, Potassium, Dolomite Powder, wheat germ, molasses … his farts were legendary, Flo … I remember once on a long drive we had to stick his bum out the window for a while … god we laughed … and the more he laughed the more he farted.

'… and then he learnt to talk, again, to see, again … learnt to go to the toilet by himself, again … dress himself, again … learnt to ride a tricycle, a bicycle, a skateboard, rollerblades, take public transport … there's a funny story there Flo …' I can tell her this stuff. '… when he was learning to take public transport I used to follow him without his knowing … I was standing on the platform one morning when his train pulled in and I saw he wasn't getting on for some reason so I yelled, 'Get on!' … he

must have thought it was the Voice of God or something, Flo …
anyway he jumped on.'

Do you remember Tiffany's Dawn Raids, Warren? 'Good
morning! Spot Inspection! Note—foster child not sleeping
in street clothes. Bedding—reasonably clean. Bathroom
and toilet facilities—adequate. Fridge—some food. Still to
provide—weekly expenditure on rent, food, entertainment,
full list of visitors to premises and Baptismal Certificate.' I
always served my emergency packet of Adora Cream Wafers
on matching Shelley Blood and Bone crockery with Floral
Motif. I was gratified to note they received an honourable
mention in more than one of Tiffany's reports. But, thank god
I had presence of mind that one particular morning she found
Luce and me in our pyjamas with our arms around each other
at the kitchen table or you'd have been back in Woodbrook
before breakfast Wassa Boy. How many times had I told you
never to let anyone in the front door before calling me? This
morning the New Little Tiffany, the one who wanted your
Baptismal Certificate, the one who tried to make me send
you to Christian Day Care in the holidays, made one of her
Spot Inspections and you just ushered her in to the kitchen.
Luce and I were having a cuddle at the kitchen table, still in
our pyjamas. New Little Tiff looked startled then Ah Ha!
Triumphant. Luce got up and walked out. Thank god, at that
moment Divine Intervention intervened and thank god Luce
looked so much like a teenage boy. I don't remember thinking
it, it just came out of my mouth, 'Young people have so many
problems these days,' I sighed, attempting what I thought was
just the right sanctimonious social worker lilt. That's when we
decided to get right out of there, go south, and this is the first
time we've been back to the pisshole of a place.

WARREN'S WORLD

'... he was so cluey, Flo, so bloody astute ... 'Do you want to see my world?' he said to one Little Tiffany as she was asking Robbie and me all these tricky questions ... he was so cute ... and there it was, the sickeningly sentimental soft centre all fascist-bureaucrats have ... she cooed ... you read that word and would never believe it but, honestly Flo, she cooed ... 'Ooh, yes Warren! I'd love to see your world.' ... he scampered in and out of his bedroom to where I'd made him a miniature world ... it was just a big board painted with green grass and blue rivers and oceans and he had dozens of miniature animals and houses and Matchbox toys and things to play with on it ... 'This is my fishie.' ... 'What's its name?' she asked ... 'It's called Pisces.' ... he scampered back and forth to his bedroom ... 'And this is my horsie.' ... 'What's its name?' ... 'It's called Equus.' ... 'This is my bulldozer.' ... 'What's its name?' ... 'Big Yellow.' ... this went on and on until, finally, he said, 'And this is my birdie.' ... 'What's its name?' she asked, literally charmed to tears ... he held it up to her in his cupped hand ... I thought, 'Enough! Enough already! You'll push it over the edge.' ... but no, he held it up to her, cupped in his dirty little paws ... 'You name it,' he said ... 'Ooh! Ooh!' she choked out between little soft sobs ... 'Let's call it—Tweetie Pie.' ... Fuck! I nearly wet myself ... I saw the sneer begin at the side of his mouth and that smug little eye roll he'd mastered ... saw them retreat and heard him whisper, 'That's a beautiful name.' ... and next time she was due to turn up I found him waiting for her outside playing with his bloody boomerang ... what an operator ... always called me 'Mum' on such occasions, Flo ... worked out those protocols himself.

'... anyway, back to his so-called *education* ... at first no school would take him ... the blinko school said he was too spaso, *Neurotic mother of a disabled child*, they wrote on the files ... thank you Freedom of Information ... and the spaso school said he was too blinko ... 'Get a hobby,' the Principal said ... what they should have said was, 'He's too Black.' ... I realise that now, it was just racism pure and simple ... it's taken thirteen years for that little brown penny to drop into this empty white skull ... I finally got him into a school for severely and multiply disabled kids with the alluring name of Multicap Meadows but when I went to enrol him, I asked the Principal what his educational philosophy was ... he proudly walked me down this long corridor past half a dozen silent classrooms full of disabled kids, stopped and said, 'Listen to that! You could hear a pin drop.' ... so, for a while, I taught him myself, at home, then got him in to one of those free schools ... that was a saga, the story of his education ... I'll tell you over a long evening by the fire, Flo ...'

And now, after all that, here we are, back in the same situation. Another little Tiffany has your future all planned, baby. Forget that TAFE music course, she told the co-ordinator you weren't an *appropriate candidate*. Why won't she back off? If they Section Nine you their Woodbrook Rotary Bush Bash Minibus won't be dropping you off to play gangsta rap with your Black bros, I can tell you that much sonny boy. No-e-no-no, it'll be driving you to the Society Workshop where they already have your name on a bench top. You'll be making coathangers for the duration, as Little New Tiff informed you the other day at your Big Case Conference, and there's not a damned thing I can do about it. I'm only your foster mother, no legal rights whatsoever, you Section Nine Ward of the State you. End of story.

runrunasfastasblahblahblah

I'VE SEEN TOO MUCH
    my life is like one of those 3D paintings
    I just keep thinking
    if only I could find the right focus, angle, perspective
    if only I could adjust my vision
    I follow the instructions
    I hold the picture close to my eyes
    I look through it so it's blurry
    I hold my gaze and slowly move it away
    I look through the picture at my own shadow
    I wait for the picture to suddenly emerge
    but it's still just an ugly mess

'Let woebegones be bygones,' Dellkeith wrote. 'Come home to us darling. We are waiting. *Dellkeith* is waiting. Your little room is waiting. The Love a Mother. The Love a Father. We paid for Experts. We took you to Authorities. Give us another go. Do you still have your lovely wavy hair, your stoop, that capillary problem with your right eye?' 'My mother's left-handed,' I told my dopey teacher but the stupid bitch just looked blank. 'It runs in the family,' Dellmay said and the stupid bitch believed her. The Gingerbread Man Syndrome I called it.

runrun as fast as you can

I used to hide in the bushes at the end of the street and watch you coming along the footpath by the railway line, 'Mumm—?' Dellmay. Walking towards me, so elegant, so beautiful, that avenue of flowering yellow Acacia blossoms tumbling down around you

a confetti of stars—falling
a cornucopia of bonbonnière—spilling.

Coming towards me in your yellow guipure lace blouse dotted with yellow seed pearls, in your hat and gloves and black suede stilettos. It made me feel funny, shy. After you passed I'd run home the back way and sit, nonchalant, legs dangling, on the fence, sick with anticipation, knowing you'd crumple onto the lounge as soon as you walked in and pulled off your shoes, peeping around the dining-room door, watching the pain on your face as you rubbed your ruined insteps, your corns, your carbuncles, your varicose veins. But why should I have been that shy with you Dellm—? … 'Mummy?' No, see, 'Mummy's' a word I can't say, even 'Mum' sticks in my throat like a wishbone.

I remember you bending down over me, Keith. Bluebellblue tumbling out of those madblue Irish eyes of yours, all over my dolls' tea party, in the cubby I'd made in the old chicken coop you'd built down the back. Sitting with my dolls amidst the old straw, pouring watertea from the English-cottage tea-set. Bending down and present-ing me with the doll's rocker you'd painted cream and appliquéd with English-cottage garden flowers.

Chicken coop.

Tea-set.

Doll's rocker.

Blue eyes.

I had to look away, shy, from your ravishing eyes. 'Dadd—?' No, see, I can't say that simple word. 'Daddy's' not a word I can say; even 'Dad' sounds soft and rotten, like a fat lie plopping out.

But I practise those words and I try to imagine them attached to some sort of feeling. But all I can see are sitcom families reading Hallmark Greeting Cards to each other.

Can I really come home to *Dellkeith* at last and feel safe?
I've never felt safe. I've never felt at home and safe. I'm barely
human.

JUST HANGING ON LIKE SHIT ON A BLANKET
        nothing in my life has made me human
        only you, Wassa Boy
        save you, save myself
        a hostage situation
        pushing you along
        in front of me
        as proof, proof, proof
        you see I had to fix something
        something had to be fixed
        save one person, save the world
        but it hasn't worked
        I've fixed nothing
        nothing's ever been fixed
        I'm not living a life
        I'm haemorrhaging a life
        the sinc(e) of the past
        blunt impact
        trauma
        traumatic bonding
        that mummydaddy thing
        looking at me with contempt
        not looking at me at all
        same as I've seen people look
        not look
        at Warren
        making an outline

around the blank space
where the body fell
I had to bury something
but it don't stay down
unless it's dead
I learnt to survive
under that look
so has he
ghosted, out of focus
in that empty space
dead space
looking into the mirror
and no face you recognise
looking back
and you develop funny methods
to survive under that look
just hanging on
like shit on a blanket

every night
when I turn out the light
I'm searching that blank face
and those empty wateryblue eyes
of blunt hate
dumb, unfocused
eyes that cut me out of the space
Dellkeith's Horrif Eye
I get real brave
I say
right up and into it
I say to it, 'You Horrif Eye'

and it just keeps coming at me
flailing its long, cruel, disgusting wind-sock lashes
trying to grab me

'every night when Daddy comes home
the monkey's on the table
get a stick and give it a poke
pop goes the weasel'

WHAT IS WRONG WITH THIS PICTURE?
Silhouetted in front of a huge black cake-hole of a railway tunnel a teenage girl in a smart school uniform stands at the very end, on the very edge of the platform. She has placed her gold-initialled brown Globite suitcase neatly beside her shiny black Clarke school shoes. She is waiting. She is waiting for the 4:46 pm train to come screaming out of that black cake-hole. She is gathering all her substantial determination and will as she waits. The train hurtles out. As the last carriage rattles past her she looks down onto the track at the outline where the body fell. She has failed—again. Again that death leaps back at her—rampant, mocking, mudbog thing. Again she catches the 5:05 pm home.

BLOOD SPREADS
Blood splatters, spreads—a Rorschach blot. A woman's hand muzzles a teenage girl's face and bashes the head again and again against a cream-painted wall. Someone is playing 'Michelle Ma Belle' at break-neck speed on an old, out-of-tune Steinway Upstanding. The blood becomes a halo of stain, a howl from a black cake-hole.

THE SINC(E) OF THE PAST—2

I only found out anything
when she'd go right off
and scream it
into the locked bedroom door
scream abuse at Keith
at me
at Nanny
at everyone and everything
shaking her pill bottles
screaming she was going to kill herself
I'd say, 'I'll bring you a glass of water then'
that was when I learnt to fight
violence with violence
that's where I learnt all I know
the Door to the Universe-ity-ity Bang Bang
I called it
screaming out for her dead babies
ghosted by her dead blue-in-the-face
diphtheria sister, May
Nanny, in those last days before
her Sudden and Mysterious Death
often mistaking Dellmay for May
'May!' she'd say, 'Oh! I mean Dellmay.'
Dell carrying around that conjoined namesake May
carrying death and loss and grief
ghosted, stalked, out of focus
still birth still birth still birth
a heritage really
runs in the family
and that's when she found out she was born dead

Nanny told me just before she died that she'd never been able to like Dellmay. Said the Doctor showed her the bumps and lumps on the baby's head and told her Dellmay would never mature beyond the age of twelve, emotionally. Said that after that she could never feel for her the way a mother should. If even your own mother doesn't like you, well—

runrunrunrun as fast as you cancancan you can't catch me I'm the blankblank Gingerbread Man

THE SINC(E) OF THE PAST—3
    the little black fruitbat
    protecting its death
    protecting everyone
    from the horror of the death
    I carried curled inside me
    like the little black fruitbat
    all leathery with feet like sticks
    like the yellow chickens' feet
    sticky-taped to Easter eggs
    I always screamed and wouldn't touch them
    protecting Dellkeith from the embarrassment
    of the dead baby
    breechscreechbirth stillborn bluebaby etiquette
    I'm sure I showed its face to her sometimes
    and that's when her pinking shear eyelashes
    cut around my dotted outline

    I have no sense of smell
    living in a glass room

inside and out
I'm a little clump
of blighted ovum
deep in the brain of the mind
all curled up there
so deepsecret
hiddenkeep

AND WHAT CAME SCREAMING OUT OF THE BIG, BLACK
CAKE-HOLE?
'People know what you are Kate. It's a wonder you can walk up
the street knowing that everyone knows what you are. A hard
closed fistofaface with a clampupyourtroublesgoodandtight-
jawedchin and not a tear neveratear for all the naughtiness
a girl who should be crying her wicked eyes out if there was
ever the sliver of a shthread of godgivendecencyandshame then
that's what we'd be seeing but then nothing nothing would
surprise me with you capableofanythingunderthesun and I'm
your mother and I know it how do you think it makes me feel to
know it to know that's what a daughter of my ownfleshandblood
could be like and I've borne it that's what I've delivered into the
world with its problems and miseries enough.'

still birth still birth still birth

and that's when I found out I was born dead

*Run. Run. As fast as you can. You can't catch me I'm the Gingerbread
Man.*

I AM A JAGGED ACHE BETWEEN TWO WALLS
    five straight sticks and one
    blow-up
    balloon
    head

    Run. Run.

    a sick child's
    stick figure
    only pain
    gives me a skin
    fills me in

    As fast as you can.

    with zig-zag
    lightning-strike
    fright-wig hair
    and a textaed
    text messaged
    plaisir
    displaisir
    plaisir
    displaisir
    clown-game
    face

    You can't catch me.

save him save myself
save him save myself

it doesn't work
it doesn't work

I'm the Gingerbread Man.

still birth still birth
still born(e) still born(e)
suppression of growth hormone
failure to thrive
she needs building up
Sustogen, Milo, Hypol, Molasses
warm-sweet milk-of-a-night
and a dose of fish tonic each morning
Bon-vita, Enos Fruit Salts, Horlicks
Cream of Yeast, Cod Liver Oil

build her up with Bon-Vita
longing for my chickens
each and everyone
to come home to roost
one roost called Mummy
one roost called Daddy
one roost called Sister
one roost called Brother
one roost called Nanny
one roost called Poppy
one roost called Child
one roost called Lover

one roost called Friend
longing for all my chickens
each and every one
to come home to roost

but if all the roosts in the coop are empty
how is it possible to be human?

chookpen and oldstraw **BLOWN TO THE FOUR–**

WHY I AM REPULSIVE. AND WHY HIM? WHY WASSA
BOY?
The little flyingfox fruitbat hung upside down in the tree in the
grass in the playground. At lunch break the boys found it and
stoned it. When its little claws lost their grip, it fell onto the
dirt, dead, bloodplum bits bitten out of its blackleather hide.

The flyingfox hung upside down in the tree. It looked
dead—all that black leathery skin folded and wrinkled, the eyes
tight shut—but it was alive. It looked evil, carnivorous, but
it was only a sweet sticky fruit and nectareous blossom eater,
crepuscular, nocturnal.

Blood-drained face, hands behind her back, retracted knees,
watching, learning, generating the rigid rules, laws, logics; the
modus operandi of a child's rule-governed, solipsistic universe
of stubborn refusal.

Shelley Blood and Bone crinolined figurine suckling a vam-
pire bat—smash—bat in a bottle of formaldehyde—smash—and
so on to the end and emptiness of the whatnot, china cabinet,
cabinet of curios—build the machine, dismantle the machine.

That's what is done to ugly, upside-down things of the night
if they show themselves to the light of day. A snarl of white and

pointed teeth in the mercurachromeorange gums—the only face the poor thing has for fear. The shiny jetbutton eyes—not evil—just frightened, panicking.

She looks down at a blood-stuffed face, at a snarl, at a torment clawing up at her.

Her face aches to achieve this contortion again after all these decades. Neuralgic the nerve, myalgic the muscle, finding and fitting into that old pincushion painpattern, that gnawbawl. Her body spasms to find the connecting nerveline. The shape that waits.

a little flexing bundle of nerve endings and openings
the strongest thing in the world
like trying to drown the Black Cat

She sleeps all the time. Sleeps down there with the dead baby. Curled around the grief and pain and death of it. A baby found finally, desiccated desert creature, mummified and leathery from under the permafrost, still with the free capital S State School milk curdled in its mouth. It is very real.

Bury it like the dead birds she found on the footpath under the electricity wires on her way home from school. Carry them and bury them in the dirt behind the chicken coop in the backyard. Wrapping them reverently in a clean pressed hankie. Bury them under a tiny rectangle of cement from the stuff she snuck out of the bag stored in the chicken coop. A paddlepopstick cross at the head and fallenfrangipani flowers—a fragrance—held down with a stick at the heart.

What should I do with it? Should I put it out of its misery? Bury it? Burn it? Mourn it? Exhume it? Find it in a Ratsak pose under the floorboards and souvenir it in a bottle of formaldehyde on a dusty schoolroom shelf? Exorcise it? Resuscitate it? Foster it?

She stuffed her rag doll with pink fibreglass from the old insulation batts, stored in the old chicken coop, and hugged into the nappy rash of its prickly heat heart, for the comfort, for the comfort. Until Keith ripped it limb from limb. Fabric fibres dangled like crepe-paper streamers from a departing ocean liner. Au revoir. Bon voyage.

I HAD TO FIX SOMETHING
>something had to be fixed
>I can't bury anything
>something has to be buried
>but it won't stay down
>unless it's dead

>paydirt—immutable rubric
>bloodweeping earth—held in the hand
>landgrab—in perpetuity
>consecrate this ground, this earth, this air, this us
>to touch is to consecrate
>do not do it lightly
>hammer it home
>tamp it down
>get stuck in
>we must eat the earth of the place we've planted ourselves
>the place they'll bury us
>it always all comes down to the land in the end
>and the earth is aboriginal

AN AERIAL SHOT OF AUSTRALIA FROM SPACE
The earth of Australia is covered with indigenous fauna woven out of cane, and painted white. There are kangaroos, emus,

goannas, snakes, dugong, turtles etc. There is the sound of a didgeridoo playing the sounds these animals make. A white hand scoops up handfuls of the white sand from the beaches that surround the continent. Each grain of sand is a white skeletal object from colonisation. There are cups, saucers, plates, vases in the shape of baskets, churches with spires, crucifixes, lockets, pianos and their musical notes, cameras, surveyors' theodolites, compasses, bar-b-qs, TV sets, old slouch hats, mobile phones, tobacco tins, crinolined figurines, bakelite dressing-table sets, shopping trolleys, stiletto shoes, clocks, fob watches, gold buttons, pearl buttons, sailing ships, false teeth, picket fences, etc. Someone has set fire to the woven cane creatures.

AN OFFICIAL LETTER

We thank you for your considerable efforts on behalf of the Department. You have been a very cost-effective way of raising a State Ward. However, we wish to inform you that the above mentioned young Torres Strait Islander Ward is scheduled to be Section Nined on the date of his forthcoming eighteenth birthday when he will pass from your remunerated foster care back into the protection of the Department of Community Services.

He has, as you'll no doubt be aware, never been legally adopted nor has he ever been under the Protection Act. Therefore, the Director of Children's Services, who is, as you would realise, his Legal Guardian, has deemed this a necessary course of action for the Welfare and Protection of both the above named Section Nine Ward and that of the community at large.

Yours sincerely ...

'Section Nined? It sounds like a cut of meat. What if I object?' I said, in my most controlled voice tone, to Little Tiff.

'Let me put it this way: as he was never legally adopted, only ever fostered, as an Officer of the Department, I have the power to forcibly remove him at any time. Let's hope it doesn't come to that.'

'To foster—to nurse, to nourish, to care for, to harbour in one's heart. And I fostered Warren,' I kept repeating to myself.

'I object!' I said.

'Then you'll have quite a fight, fight, fight on your hands,' replied Little Tiff.

runrun all over the place but they'll still get you

Get another drink. 'Stewardess. Another whisky. Thanks.'

THE APARTHEID VOICE CHOIR (AVC) SINGS 'THE APARTHEID DREAM'

His family chucks him out. His people chuck him out. Do they know something that you don't? How do you think it makes his family feel, hey? Bringing him back to lay at their feet like a dog with a long-buried corpse in its mouth. You just waltz in with a big stupid smile on your dial, 'Haven't you forgotten something?' Home Alone. You shame them!

Listen to us.

You've stolen him, stolen him from his heritage. Institutional Abuse. Protection. Surveillance. Monitoring. Assessment. Testing. Interviewing. Processing. Assessing. Control. Fulfilling his Destiny. File Thick as a Fist. Good-morning Spot Inspection.

Why have you shaved half his hair off?

His family chucked him out, his people chucked him out. Survivors. Hunter-gathers. Subsistence gardeners. Fishers. Maybe they were wiser and kinder than you. Just imagine letting him go. Feel how easy it would be to just go with the flow. Stop struggling against the current. Listen to the whispering voices of your whiteness. Listen to us, the Apartheid Voice Choir, the AVC. Everyone, even Warren, is showing you the way, why fight it? No one will blame you, say you've failed. You've done everything, more than you should have, actually, and we think you know that as well as the next. What right did you have to stand between him and his fate, the inevitability of his predicament? Perhaps he, on some level, knows he must, finally, in this lifetime, live out that fate, that place, his place in history and the history of his people. Just let him go. Doesn't he have the right to work out his own little bit of history, his own karma shall we say? Cut your losses. Cut his losses. Let History, Fate, Inevitability loose. Let them loose. Stop your stinking Will. They'll take over in the end anyway.

I give Warren a letter I've written. I try to talk to him. He just acts dumber and dumber out of anger, aggression, resistance towards me. He hates me. 'Well I hate you too sonny boy.' He goes to bed outside in the yard in the dark in a chicken coop. 'I won't be cooped up inside,' he says. He demands to sleep out there and eat from a dog's bowl. It's a defiant, aggressive, victim, abused-child statement he wants to make, to live. He's found the shape that waits, and nestles in. I go to some Authority, some Kind Figure for help, advice. He's the Choir Master. I ask if he's read Warren my letter. He says it's over there. It's burning in a potbellied stove sort of thing made of dirty old tin cans. The Kind Figure grabs me and pushes my head into a forty-four gallon drumful of water. He hates me too. He wants to drown me. I struggle and get away. I am defiant.

The AVC gets quite vicious, more threatening towards me. The Choir Master holds me up by one rag-doll arm as an exhibit. I feel like a kid being held up in front of the whole school on parade. The AVC hangs off his every word, wrapped, hypnotised, dead-eyed, blank. He 'sings' to his choir:

The essence of Nature is change. Everything must change or die. It's our turn now. Leave her alone for now. We can let her live, speak—for now—for this time because, at this moment, we must change or die. So, we change because we don't want to die, do we?

This Choir Master has something like a goitre under his chin. It's a mini-me of himself, a sort of homunculus baby Jesus/ Gingerbread Man. It's Warren. He's slicing bits off and feeding it to these people, this choir, these devils of hate and silencing. They're gobbling it up like a tasty treat. He's eating a slice himself.

I wonder, 'Does Christ take the Eucharist himself? Your turn. U-Christ. U-turn.'

Why do you hate me?

And the sung reply of that ardent choir, *Because you put an oh-so-kindly-Christian face on Hate. Stand in the way of Fate. Fate working, Fate willing, Fate working itself out in the world, to its logical end. Your Salvation Arrogance. But he'll find his way back to where he belongs. We all know where he belongs. He knows where he should be. His history. He's history. His his-try working itself out. While we watch. Let's watch!* they squeal in gleeful chorus.

Second verse. *The luxury of your affluence. It would have been far kinder to have let him get used to the way of life in the Home years ago. Instead, now it will be dreadful for him at first, till he readjusts. There's no doubt about that. But they were purpose-built for that type of thing. You think you're some sort of hero; people think you're a fool. Crazy. Even his own family can't fathom it. Crazy white ways. How do you think it makes them feel? Hey!*

Why do you hate me?

For barging in where you weren't welcomed or wanted. Are you ever welcomed or wanted? What kind of a do-gooder, white, liberal, Christian, bargerinerer, making-matters-worserer are you?

Why do you hate me?

Because you're not one of us and you should be. Because you are and you won't accept it. Because you're such a goody-two-shoes. Because you're ridiculous in your phoney-baloney innocence. What illness was it? What illness was it, do you think, made him halt and blind, a sucker for the healing hands of Jesus? Made him available for anyone, even a fuck-up like you, to lay their healing hands upon? Because you're wilfully stubborn. Because no one has the right to stand against Fate, History, Inevitability working itself out while we watch. That's our job. Because you had the hubris, the stubbornness, the sheer wilfulness (but you called it nicer names). You put an oh-so-kindly-Christian face on your own Hate so you could stand in the way of Fate. Because you're in a Hell of your own perverse making. Because you're ridiculous and you don't know it. Throwing your whole body into the machinery.

They're right! What if they're right? They're right!

You hate him and—He. Does. Not. Love. You. He's seen the alcoholic, lesbianism's-a-white-disease dyke mess that Lucille

*made of you. He's threatened to dob you in to little Tiff, hasn't
he? Nice going Sunshine.*

Warren hates me. He's ashamed of me and made fun of me
to his Black mates and to his white mates on that TV program.
He even hates Flo calling me 'Mum'.

*He despises you, doesn't he? And he can't get away from
you and you won't ditch him. He despises you because we are
whispering in his heart and he hears us. He despises you for all
your Devotion and Care, all your Worrying and Advice, your
Love and Nagging. He knows what it really amounts to. Miss
Miss-ion Manager. All the times he was forced and coerced into
saying 'yes' and do as he was told. He despises you because we're
whispering all the stories of the other mothers, his real mothers.
The abuses and the rapes, the removals and the broken hearts
and broken lives and anguished wailing. When he looks at you
he sees the Enemy. And you've insisted he smile and cohabit.*

*You despise yourself because you know we're right. In fact,
we don't exist, this is you, yourself, speaking to you, yourself.
This is your Australianness. Take stock. Reconsider. You're
turning yourself inside out for him. He's turning himself inside
out for everybody else. But you're being given another chance
here. They'll take him off your hands. There's no other way.
No one would blame you. It's for the best. For his own good.
We've given you fair warning. Listen to us! Warren wants to
reclaim his birthright. Doesn't he love telling that story of his?
He's fitting into the shape that waits. And you want to reclaim
your birthright. Come on, slip back into that old slipstream.
An easy ride. He can still reclaim his Birthright. There's a nice
warm plot in a nice safe institution waiting for him when he
turns eighteen. The staff is all in place. The mini-bus is all
fuelled up. He'll be Happy-as-Larry. You know he will. And*

he'll be Safe. He's the White Man's Burden. Put down that Burden. Cut your losses and—Let. Fate. Loose. We know how much you want to.

He knows all this. They are his stories and he's repeated most of them any number of times to anyone who'll listen. Casting you in a number of wicked, white stepmother roles. He loves telling his story. He's Authentic when he's telling it. Everyone believes him. He loves the Sympathy. Moving people to tears. The deep satisfaction of the narrative form, the palpability of the narrative force moving through our lives, sucking us into itself. The potted version of the tragedy, told with feeling, 'doing an Oprah'. The audience response. The Authentic Audience Response. The Guilt. The Tears. The Sentiment. The free flow of emotions. The warm Laughter. It's Heart-warming. It's Heart-wrenching. It's 'telling it from the heart', that's what he's been told being 'Abadigenous', as he calls it, means, is. It's one of his greatest pleasures and a release from you. He escapes your rigour (mortis) truth. He betrays you every chance he gets and the crowd loves it. When-did-you-stop-beating-your-wife? And they are happy, oh so happy, to believe him and fuss over him as they slice him another piece of the Cake. But, don't worry, we don't hold anything against you, we're All White down here. Why should you worry what a sick, spaso, blinko, dumbo, low-caste, low-life boong retard mud thinks of you? You're pathetic. He's human garbage. Everyone's tried to throw him out.

Now let us sing:

> *I am a baby Aryan*
> *not Jewish or sectarian*

and I have no plan to marry
an ape or a Rastafarian
Ozzie, Ozzie, Ozzie
Oy! Oy! Oy!
Mozzie, Mozzie, Mozzie
Scratch! Scratch! Scratch!

I hate Warren. I hate him for showing me up to myself. My coy, closet Christianity. Hate him because he's the focus for all the abuse and filth that's been directed at me, because I chose him to hold up against that as proof of some pudding and now he's the conduit for it. Hate him because I see what that violence has turned him into. The Stolen Generation's just the most recent story in a long epic. Some Christian re-enactment. Save him. Save myself. Hate him because it hasn't worked. I'm lost. I'm part of this Crusade, this maelstrom of involution. Everything is regressing, going back to some equilibrium, some point of origin. Hell spreads.

'You want to hear me say it don't you? OK! I. Wish. I. Had. Just. Left. Him. There. To. Die.'

just run

When will this flight end? When will the 'Buckle Seat Belts' sign ding on? When will we land and taxi down the runway?

God, I need another drink. 'Stewardess—'

I'm walking into a carpark at night. There's an old Black man, an elder, hiding behind some cars. He aims his spear at me and I hear it whoosh past me. I have done something wrong. I am guilty of some crime. I am under sentence. I have been judged. He has come to carry out sentence. He says, 'Payback'. I say, 'Safeways'.

I dream I'm in a James Bond movie. Savage dogs are chasing me. They want to tear my throat out. I've seen too much and they know I will talk.

I feel myself slipping into Amnesia. All the stories of my life slipping away. I am his guardian. I cannot leave my post. Sometimes I think if they just took Warren away I'd forget about him in a week. Slip back into that old slipstream. An easy ride, a birthright. Every voice is saying, 'Give it away, girlie.' And every fibre in my being is screaming, 'Hang on! Don't let him slip through those holes in the net! After all these years, after all you know about him, don't let them do it to him!' People don't ask after him. Dellkeith never asks after him. Never sends him Christmas or Birthday presents. I dream I'm a child again. I've been given a huge Gingerbread Man as a Christmas present. I am disgusting myself as I chew off, then swallow, each limb, then I crunch into the head and finally the body itself.

I've left him in the frozen food section of the supermarket. I'll pick him up if he's still there when I come back next week. He's lying in the gutter after a road accident. I'll call the ambulance if he's still there when I come past next month. He sits in silent agony while his teeth are extracted, without anaesthetic. I'll insist on painkillers if he's still there when I open my eyes.

I've eaten him. I've swallowed him. He's suffocating inside me. He wants out.

I find an old shoebox in the rubbish. I take the lid off and see it's full of sick, disabled and amputee children. He's there in a wheelchair, smiling up at me. The diabetes has taken a hold and he's had his legs amputated. Then I notice all the kids are Black. I wish I hadn't found the box. I want to throw it back.

run run running on empty now for years

A child is kept, curled up on straw, in a small wooden fruitbox. The chicken-wire lid latches closed, twisted over a bent and rusty nail. It's like a rabbit hutch. There's a scrap of faded blue towelling on top of the chicken wire. At the bottom of the box, around the four sides, runs a polished brass plaque which is finely engraved in ornate copperplate with the words, 'A Safe Place From Which A Child May Be Allowed To View The Sky.'

I just dream on and on. Will this plane never land?

I am running across a steel bridge, a stone bridge, a wooden bridge, a bamboo bridge, a rope bridge. It cannot take my weight. Then I look down. Uh! Oh! My legs are pumping thin air. I am a cartoon character. Uh! Oh! I'm the Roadrunner just before he falls—splat.

Thank god. We're landing.

One—collect luggage. Two—taxi to *Dellkeith*. Three—sober up, breathe. Four—keep sobering up, keep breathing. Five—say hello to Dellkeith. Six—taxi to hospital. Seven—say hello to Flo. Eight—oh shit. Nine—breathe. Ten—keep breathing.

THE APOLOGIA

I want to tell you Flo, Mum, tell you, look, I haven't made much of a fist of mothering him, either

I'm sorry I can't protect him from myself and all I stand in for, I thought I could

I'm sorry you never knew him while he was growing up, he was a fabulous kid

I'm sorry I don't understand what happened and why he ended up in Cherrymead and with me

46

I'm sorry I just went silent and awkward and didn't know what to say to you when you called me 'Mum' on the phone

I feel awful about that

I'm sorry I've got no idea what you're talking about when you talk about Islander adoption

I'm sorry I'm so scared of you and your family that I have nightmares about meeting you—all those Black faces staring at me

I'm sorry I don't know any other way to be with you than stiff-backed and suspicious, the whiteness rising up in me

I'm sorry that something made him halt and blind a sucker for the healing hands of Jesus, made him available for anyone, even a fuck-up like me, to lay their healing hands upon

I'm sorry I haven't been a better mother, just look at the mess I've made. I haven't been able to fix anything. It's all going into auto-reverse.

I'm sorry that I've hardly got any photos of him growing up to show you

I'm sorry you're dying and he'll never get to really know you

I'm sorry I can't let him go home with you yet

I'm sorry I'm going to have to try to ask you to help us and worry you when you're so sick

I'm sorry I don't know how to do it

I'm sorry I said nothing when Tiffany told me she'd told you he was a vegetable

I'm sorry I said nothing when she told me she'd told you you should be grateful that some do-gooder was stupid enough to want him

I'm sorry I said nothing when she told me all you'd want was money anyway

I'm sorry I believed her

I'm sorry we don't have any common ground, any terra firma, to stand on together to help him

And now I'm sick of apologising. Of minding my words and mincing matters. Of trying and trying to protect the little shit from himself and from all I stand in for. Of judging and condemning myself. Sick of just hanging on.

But I'm his guardian and I won't leave my post. I'm the ever-ready Eveready and I'll never say die.

WARREN

A TORTURING DREAM
(English language title)

SORPEKLAM TEPERDA KO TEGMI
(Meriam Mer—Eastern Islands language title)

WADTHI PIKI
(Kala Lagaw Ya—Western Islands language title)

If Torres Strait languages
become extinct or
the culture becomes
pure contemporary,
our grip with our land
will be loosened,
our identity will become
a torturing dream
in the future.

EPHRAIM BANI

'Escuse I, Bud. Scuse I lady. Got all these things. Stow it don't throw it, hey! Sorry about the hold up but those Scrutiny Guards thought I was on something and they wouldn't let us on the plane but you can't OD on OJ can you? Kate reckons it's a wonder I'm not orange instead of Black I guzzle so much of the stuff. Man to man, they reckoned Mum there, Kate, must be one of them, you know, prosatutes—but they used a worse word—to be with a 'drunk boong.' Little Miss Mummy Fix-it went right off, fixed things like she usually does, with yellin which, as you know, don't fix nothin. She's right off circuit sometimes. Man! They pointed their guns at us and everything but they had to apologise too after I told em I'm a bit wonky from me disability. I've been listening to their 'Oh, sir, we're so sorry. We're so sorry.' I kept up the atmosphere though, as usual. Sang 'Ebony and Ivory' to em. That got em laughing. Reckon they're gunna call me Mr Stevie Wonder from Down Under from now on.

'Escuse all the messin around and stops and starts Bud. I'm makin a tape letter here on me new Walkman that Sir gave me and I'm just gettin the hang of. It's me first ever letter to me mother, me real mother, who I talked to on the phone for the first time since I was a bub, the other day. She's me real mother who I haven't seen since I was as high as a knee, and she, that Kate over there, stole me off of her to pretend she is me mother, so you'll be hearing me whistlin and singin and playin me didg for the tape to endatain her in her hospital bed where she is at the moment.

'That's the family whistle you just heard me do there Bud. Everyone on the Island's got one and so you know who's comin before you even see em in the dark.'

'... thanks for that family whistle there Mum ... now I know what it feels like, I just showed it to the Bud beside me here in flight and told him a bit a culture, Islander-style ... wish Dad'd been there to have a word with the other night but you gave me his name and now I know he's Albert and I'll see him same time as seeing you so no probs on that score ... so, good morning there Mum relaxin back in your hospital bed ... and good mornin here Dad too if you're sittin there with her and also any bros or bulas or couses ... I'm DJing this letter for you high in the blue, blue sky before I can do it live in-personating meself.

'... all right! tunin in here to Warren, also known as Was-A-Boy-Now-A-Man, also known as Mr Racket and now me updated Abadigenous name AAD, Albert-After-Dad ... Kate says to wait and talk to me Mum before changing me name ... she's really losin it Mum, she **is** me Mum ... jeez! ... anyway thanks for the cool-up rattle Mum and Dad ... I've got it here clipped to me belt ... I can play it already cause it's in me Islander blood memory.'

'Aahg! Aagh! Ha! Ha! Ha! That got ya didn't it Bud? It always gets em at parties too cause I blend so well in the dark.'

'... sorry about that Mum and Dad ... the joke's lost on you cause this is a tape but if we were on videophone you'd see me big Black mugshot going 'Aah!' with me big white teeth and eyes flashin in the dark cause the lights just went off ... scary as a spook in that Ghost Train at Luna Park Kate and I like so much ... scared the guy beside me half to deaf but he got the joke.'

'Didn't ya Bud? Hang on, I'll just wipe that. Kate ud says it's not a polite in-joke.'

'... and yes Mum, it's hard to be pretty in this ugly city ... got meself a special old-time T. I. hair-do Mum ... you'll love it ... Kate hates it, of course ... it's a died hair skull-ture painted grey and green and white—Abadigenous Islander flag colours, the sis who did it reckoned and she reckons it's hair skull-ture cause half me head's shaved and that's the bit that's green—cool.

'... like I was sayin Mum, long time no see, me bein one of those blinkos—that's a blind joke Mum—in a bunch of Sundays ... lucky you fed me some of that wild, wild wonky berry before they took me off the Island cause here I am, back like a boomerang or, like Kate says, back like a bad smell ... Kate told me that you loved me and that, but it was cause of health reasons you sent me away ... but maybe you fed me a bit too much of that wonky berry if you don't mind me sayin that to you Mum and Dad, and that's why I'm a bit wonky on me feet and in me eyes and brain ... sorry about that Mum and Dad but no offence meant and no offence taken ... here's a song Sir taught me I know you'll like ... I'll sing-a-long gettin into the act karaoke-style.

'old T. I. my beautiful home
it's the place where I was born
where the moon and stars that shine
make me longin for home
old T. I. my beautiful home'

Woo!

'... sorry about that ugly noise there Mum ... it was me air iconiser getting out of hand ... Sir reckoned every Islander should have one so we can carry the sea air around with us all the time ... Sir bought me a sarong and a plastic palm to go with it and when he turns his heater way up, man I could be at home ... he knows all about bein a T. I. seein as he was a teacher up there for years ... made a good joke with him the other day Mum ... once you get to know me you'll know I like jokes ... got him really laughin ... you say, 'How do you know I'm a T. I.?' ... they say, 'I don't know, how?' ... then you put a tea bag on your eye ... get it? ... even got Kate laughin at that one.

'... we should go on *This is Your Life* Mum ... they can show us all sittin on the sand under the stars eatin coconut-ice and pineapple rings and wreck-and-silly ate-ing with some of your famous La Cook-a-racha cookin you told me about, that's still buried in the hot stones, and be free and happy walkingabout singin and dancin the hoola hoola ... but no more wonky berries this time thanks Mum ... Kate ull be a bit sad for a while after seein me on TV ... and I'll miss our favourite Friday night yarns and spaghetti bolognaise with as much parmesan cheese as I can handle ... yeah ... I'll miss that a bit ... but she says I can't go Black cause she's tryin to make me white like her ... I have to wash all the time and use that deodorant and clean me teeth and keep me nose clean and that's cause maybe she reckons Blacks smell ... and she's always tryin to ruin my Black Mind Power by makin me use one of those diary organisers from the Blinko Sociation Mum, but us Blackfellas don't need to write stuff down do we? ... we got oral stories, that's what I heard, and that's what's our culture, to yarn a lot, right Mum? ... Kate's always tellin me what to do Mum ... she tried to stop me yarnin about me this-is-your-life in TVland cause she said it was lyin and bullshit ... if you'll pardon the lingo ... but the TV Man, that Inta Viewa, loved me yarnin, so it can't be lyin ... he told me that when you yarn from the heart you tell the Abadigenous truth ... and that's what I said in person-ating meself on TV, so there you go, end of discussion ... that's what I saw on TV, anyway.

'... Kate's always sayin, 'Keep your nose clean, stop runnin away or you'll be Awarded the State for the rest of your life ... the Department wants to take you away and keep you un-Protected, forever ... it's Aussie Rules ... I won't be able to fix it.'

'... she's always sayin, 'If you just tell me I can fix it' but, really, she can't fix nothin that matters ... no way, man! no way! ... one thing I gotta have is me freedom ... I've gotta roam free and smell the gum trees and sea breeze.

'... sorry about that Mum ... that was a blast from me didg that I use to calm meself down ... me Mind Screens were goin bad like hell ... if you'll pardon the lingo there ... I'll just wipe that ... gotta keep up the atmosphere for you there in hospital, hey .... hey! this yarn'll give you a good laugh Mum ... the cops picked me up the other day ... 'Blow into this son,' one of em said ... you have to talk real slow and careful to em sometimes cause some of em have that brain slowness and a sort of speech pediment ... 'Just-blow-into-this-son,' he goes ... so I did ... and pop, clink, clink, clink ... and those crystals flew everywhere ... circular breathin from playin the didg ... 'Are they the right colour, Protective?' I asked ... he was real quiet, didn't say nothing ... me Mind Screen was shakin like a leaf ... 'Are they the right colour, Detective?' I asked real loud and careful ... and that's when he started thumpin me ... you pick me up when I'm runnin, you pick me up when I'm walkin, you pick me up when I'm bloody standin still, Mr Protective, Mr Protective,

Mr Protective Sir ... fair dinkum, it's a pretty funny way to treat a guy, isn't it Mum?'

'See ya Bud.'

'... that was the Bud beside me stretchin his legs Mum ... Mum, I just had to do a bolt and go out into Mother Nature and hear the birds and the bees and the flowers and the trees and the water and sit under a Cool Bar tree with me Cool-up rattle and eat Bushman's tucker from a bag and have a bit uv a wild think-tank for meself—like Kate always says, 'Go and think about it for a wild' ... so I went up bush to the bush suburbs to this big Woodbrook Shopping Town Mall that I know ... for a bush suburb it isn't even a garden suburb ... like I told the social worker at the Big Case Con-far-ance about me Kate took me to last week ... I told that social worker when she said she wanted me to go to live in Woodbrook ... I said, 'Well, the problem is there's no wood and also there's no brook, end of story' ... and I was buskin me didg ... yeah! I'm a professnull didg player you can tell Dad ... you'll love this one Mum! ... I was doin real well and that but then this racket starts up and the Shopping Town Scrutiny Guard—Sir—comes up and says, 'It's Wreck-and-silly-ate-em Week next week son. It's Japanese Week this week.' 'Ah so! Saki Teriaki,' I said ... and anyway that got him laughin and Sir's a real nice bloke when he takes his uniform and gun off ... Sir ... he likes me to call him 'Sir' ... anyway, Sir bought me this Walkman and he showed me this really good hostel ... only $11 for all you can eat and a bed for the night ... better than sleepin like a sandwich in Cardboard Town under the starry, starry sky ... lots of stew and buns with icin on from yesterday and some people that talk to you a lot and some people that don't talk at all ... some of em know this city better than Public Transport ... some of em are a bit off circuit and I had to give one young fella a bit of a talkin to about the grog cause his Mind Power was goin all wrong with it … reckoned I couldn't be a real bro if I didn't get charged up with him … I said, 'Listen here Bud, no fear, don't offer me none of that. I got diabetics and I bet you have too. You'll wonder why you'll die but you know it's the drink. You know what that does to your Mind Power and if there's one thing us Blackfellas uv got really, really strongly it's that Mind Power.' … he called me a mud mask? … fair dinkum! it's a pretty funny way to see a guy isn't it Mum?' Escuse I for a minute Mum.'

'Hello! State Ward 54321 Blast-off speaking. Yeah! I'm inflight. Just makin a tape to send to Mum in the hospital and keepin up the atmosphere here in company class. And remember—it's hard to be pretty in this ugly city—but **you** are, Miss Rachael. Keep that one in mind when you're out and about, Miss You Miss Rachael. Miss R? Miss R?' Lost her.

'… in case you were wonderin, that noise was me mobile goin off, Mum … another present from Sir … that was me girl-friend, Rachael, from the hostel … we're engaged … I met her on Platform Six … she was stranded there and settlin in for the night cause she'd lost her ticket and was afraid of gettin through the barriers … I know those barriers well, so I helped her … she's a bit slow in her brain patterns … but I tell you what, she got through the barriers of me heart alright … since me little sweetheart Lisa died I've been a bit lonely to tell you the truth Mum … that little lady taught me everythin I know about sex down there in the adventure playground after school … we were going to get married and everythin … she knew all about it … I'd like to have a woman and that … sorry Mum … Kate'd say that's not propriate talk … anyway, I reckon Rachael's just my size … cool but not froz-en … Kate's always tryin to fix me but Rachael likes me bein just who I am right now ... whenever she sees me she sings out that pin-ball song to me ... 'that deaf, dumb, blind kid sure plays a mean pin-ball' ... ye-ha! Timezone Tommy—that's what she calls me—the best player ever ... Kate says sex is natural and that but, to tell you the truth Mum, she just keeps sayin it but I want to say how is it natural and OK? ... to tell you the truth Mum, sex terror-fries me ... sorry about that sort of talk again there Mum.'

'Reckon I'll wipe all that, hey lady?'

'... geez! I'm too popular Mum ... there it goes again, escuse I.'

'State Ward 54321 Blast-off on the flip side of the blower here. Just ring that Legal Eagle, Rach. I gave you the number. It's on the triangalar folded piece of paper in your purse. You're over eighteen, Rach, they can't force you nowhere after that and I don't care what Kate over there says, I'll do what I want. Free Willy, everythin. I'm not a kid nomore either.'

'... sorry about that interruption again there Mum ... now where was I? ... oh yeah! they call me Racket, Mum ... that's me nicked name ... the TV Man who made the TV program you saw called me a Real Racketeur cause I make such a racket when I tell me yarns ... I made em laugh and I made em cry on that program, didn't I Mum? ... Kate called me a great big Christmas hamper for doing that.

'... that Inta Viewa—but really he was the man sitting across from me—asked me how I learnt to play didgeridoo from me grandfather sitting under a big Cool Bar tree eating Bushman's tucker from a bag ... and he asked me how I felt about being stolen ... and he really really listened ... and got really upset when I told him about that white woman coming and stealing me from my tribe who didn't want me and threw me in the garbage tip cause I was handicapped … and he asked me if I ever ran away and I told him about how I always kept running and running away from that gubba to get back to my tribe … and she chased me and chased me through the rain and cold and I was just running and running and driving that doggie-gem car in me wet nappy and crying to get back to me mother … he asked me if I remembered us all sitting together and singing and dancing around the camp fire … and I told him about how I could see us all on me Mind Screens sitting together and laughing and singing and dancing the hoola hoola around the camp fire before that foster mother grabbed me when she caught me and how she was just laughing and laughing all the time at me and took me away from all the other little children who were also crying and sick and then kept me by meself with her and cooped me up in a chicken coop down the back and that's why I can't be cooped up nowadays cause I remember that horrible place … and he was really interested when I told him about how she tried to make me wash myself all the time and clean my teeth and use deodorant and stuff because she hates the way Black people smell and she wants to make me white like her … he said that's what's called Similar Relationsist Genderslide so it's got a name there … she put smelly stuff on me legs so I couldn't walk and made me push meself around with me hands on a piece of wood with wheels and I got stones and dirt in the palms of me little hands all the time and sometimes she stuck big needles in me back and they hurt so much I can still feel em goin in and she always kept makin me take lots of tablets that tasted awful and got stuck in me little throat sometimes and she yells at me all the time and takes all the money the Gubberment gives her but it's supposed to be for me and she doesn't even feed me—much … Kate was really upset when I said that …

cause she makes really good spaghetti bolognaise every Friday Family Together Night ... that TV Man told me it was a film I was in but really, when Kate saw it at that castacrew screenin, she cried and said it wasn't a film, it was a doctored-mentality ... and that's when I took off, did a real bolt that night ... can't remember where I went but Kate, of course, got the cops on me and they took me in roughly and took me back to Kate who, of course, cried and cried, as usual.'

'I'll wipe all that. It'll just upset Mum again. Don't you reckon lady?'

'... me didg here could really tell you how I felt talkin to you on the phone the other night Mum ... man! I just can't talk about it ... me Screens go all wobbly and really loud and then really quiet Mum so I'll just play it for you now till me Screens go back to normal and it'll show you how I feel a bit.'

'Need to stretch your legs too lady? I'll save your seat, no worries.'

'... I'm feelin a bit bad actually Mum, to tell you the truth ... can I ask you one thing that's a bit hard to ask, and proberly a bit hard to answer? ... why did you send me away? ... were you ashamed of me bein a bit wonky? ... no offence meant there Mum and no offence taken, just askin ... so, anyway, I'll play you this song on me didg, Mum, all tucked up in hospital there ... bet you wish it was with Dad and not with that Diabetics ... just kiddin ... us Islanders joke most when we're saddest, so you're watchin me learnin to be an Abadigenous Islander here Mum and Dad ... I been tucked up with that Diabetics meself so I'm a real Islander too and I didn't just get toes off like you said you did, I nearly had me whole leg ampertatered with gang-of-green-you-moan-you-off-the-bone, or something ... Kate never stops tryin to take me Blundies off to check me toes now.

'If you could be in **my** shoes for just one day you'd see some things Mum, Kate, Mum ...'

'... but this is me didg talkin to you now Mum ... all you need to know about a didg is how to listen.

'... sorry! I got a bit of anger in there ... this bus driver confracated me Blinko Pass yesterday cause he said I wasn't blind and I mustuv stolen it ... just grabbed it and pushed me off the bus ... well Mum, that's OK cause I've got size 13 feet, like you told me Dad had and I must take after him cause I'd rather walkabout on em everywhere, and so I just walked those size 13 Blundies all the way back to the city ... but, fair dinkum, it's a funny way to treat a guy ... don't worry about me though Mum, I've got these Helpers with me all the time ... one of them's called Public Transport ... he's always around and he showed me how to get back to the city ... he's a bit like the green man on the Walk sign and he calls up me Mind-Screen maps ... 'Number 73. The 6:55. Express. No stops to Woodbrook.' ... me Screens have been goin a bit blurry though, especially the one I call There-Before-You-Talk ... the blue one ... that one's hard to see cause the sky's nearly exactly exactly the same blue and I have to really really concentrate to see him ... I tried to show Mum, sorry Mum, me other Mum, her Help-hers ... I told her, 'You've got to concentrate and whisper softly to yourself and that way they come sometimes. They make a noise like pss, pss, pss.' ... her Help-hers would help her too, if she let em, but she always wants to do it alone, so that's it ... they can't do nothin about her with that attitude ... that white one, Be-Kind, told me, 'Try, but you know what she's like.' ... Be-Kind told me that she only had black and white screens, which doesn't help.

'... Mum, me other Mum, Mum, Aunty Kate, she's real shaky, and I have to keep a joke or two up all the time to keep up the atmosphere ... she doesn't take her time talkin to people and doesn't let people have some time to talk back for themselves and that's what causes the trouble ... she doesn't keep up no atmosphere and they don't have time to blend in ... that's why when she talks to people and talks the wrong way it doesn't blend into the other person's mind ... it just bounces off the other person's mind like a trampoline ... poing! poing! ... see, if she loses all her friends and family and me, say, and gets stuck somewhere towards the future, she won't have nothing to back her up ... I told her that and that's a very powerful line that one ... if you walk a good long way amongst free-range flowers you're goin in the right direction ... always go towards the atmosphere cause if you go the wrong way you're goin towards hell.

'... but sometimes those two who pretend to be Helpers try to twist me ... they're both red and white and have blue faces in sharp cross shapes you wouldn't like Mum ... and it's a bit hard to get rid of em if Public Transport don't know the layout so much ... that's why I have to take off sometimes cause I have to find the water to lose those two cause they really really follow me and I can only lose em when I go down to the water cause it's like a mirror maze to them all that water and sky and they get lost ... but I don't know where the water is up here so, soon as we land, I'm gunna have to do a bit of a bolt again for a while and find it, Mum ... but that's somethin you'll have to keep mum about Mum ... there it goes again.'

'Yo! Rachael. Nothin I can do about that up here like a bird in the sky, darlin. No! Don't go home with em. Say like we practised. 'I'm over eighteen.' Yeah, that's right, like that. And— and— go on. What else? 'And even though I'm not a kid no more it's still kidnappin and you can't make me come with you and this is the name and phone number of me Legal Eagle.'

That's it. You got it. And then hand em that triangalar piece of paper. Gotta love ya and leave ya, Rach. They don't like us usin mobiles in the plane darlin. Call you when I get there.'

'… another sorry about that Mum … my fiancée again … she's twenty-two yeah! an older woman … and nothin her parents can do cause she wanted to come and live with me in the hostel … but they won't let us live in the same room in the hostel cause they're Christians there … I feel a bit sorry for those Christians Mum … they don't seem to have no friends … not like me, I got lots … they come in to see me **all** the time to talk and give me free books and things … I talk to them a bit cause they must be pretty lonely and I take the little books cause I don't want to be rude but I can't even read em … they're prayin for me, Mum, cause they said I'm a Pagan but I told em I'm not in that band no more cause of how they treated me but they still want to pray for me anyway which is real nice of em … they said it's the Christian Rule about Bedrooms why Rach and I can't sleep together … they gave her the room next to me and I can hear her on the other side of the wall all night, sad and cold and missin me and so she curls up on the floor with her blanket and pillow with her ear to the wall, and I make her sleep easy playin me didg right up against the wall … I play it really, really softly like this Mum so, if you're lyin there and can't sleep, it might make you sleep easy too, listenin … geez! there she is again.'

'No Rach I can't bring home no fish and chips. I told you I'm in the air. You'll have to go yourself. Get what you usually get Rach. I don't know Rach, it's up to you. Salt. No salt. Vinegar. No vinegar. Tell you what, buy the fish and chips plain then buy a packet of salt and a bottle of vinegar and mix and match as much as you like and when I come back I can add as much spice as I like too. Problem solved! No problems. See ya.'

'... that was me sweet little girl again Mum with a fish and chips problem that I solved for her ... she's got one of those very very low IQs Mum cause they didn't die-a-nose her blood problem at birth ... we're getting married on her twenty-third birthday ... Sir said we could live with him in the same bedroom cause he's not a Christian but he's a Bachelor with Bachelor Ways and I don't think Rach would approve ... her parents sent the cops lookin for her and she was on TV as missin and everything ... but she wasn't missin nothin ... the hostel people rang the cops but she's over eighteen so what could they do? ... her parents reckon she's getting section nined same as Kate reckons I am ... so I told her that would be good because we can still be together if we're both put in Section Nine ... we'd like to have babies but I said, 'Rachael if you can't get off Platform Six by yourself how will you look after a little one?'... so that made her sit up and have a wild think more clearly than usual ... and I know about those conception things that I use ... and she said, 'Anyway, you can't have bubs without a job.' ... which is true ... but I could get a job doing lots of things ... firstly, there's no money in music ... that Koorie band named The Black Pagans wouldn't even pay me when I asked ... they just laughed ... they only let me play in the breaks when they went off with their girlfriends or when they were too pissed or stoned ... anyway, I reckon it's cause I'm not a Koorie like them, I'm an Abadigenous Islander, and they mentioned that a lot ... and I mentioned it back after they wouldn't give me no money ... they never even give me nothing, not even for a taxi home at midnight ... so that's it for them ... I'm better off just buskin ... keep me own hours ... keep me own money ... stay free like Willy.

'... or ... I could be a DJ, I've got enough CDs ... or ... I could be a counsellor cause I've got the right attitude ... see, most counsellors want to put everything down on paper before they'll even talk to you but the thing they don't see is that paper doesn't talk and they've forgotten how to listen to the person who is sitting-opposite-them ... and those sort of people don't know nothin about the atmosphere ... don't know nothin about their Helpers ... know what I mean Mum ... they're actually the person sittin opposite you but they think, they think Mum, and I can view this on me Mind Screen, they think in their heads, that they're sittin on top of you so that's when the talking down to you starts and that's where the trouble with come-una-kate-shun starts ... see, if they could be in my shoes for a while they might see some things full frontal ... to come-una-kate you have to sit opposite with people and talk across for a wild but most of those counsellors won't let nobody sit opposite ... just cause they have all the right words don't mean they're right ... Kate doesn't like it when I tell her that ... I can see how people really feel on me Mind Screens and I know how to fix em up if they'll listen a bit ... that's why I reckon I should be one of those counsellors for me work.

'... my Lisa came back to see me the other night Mum, talkin about counsellin ... she came screaming up to me through the floor boards callin out to me ... I said, 'Lisa, you're better off down there darlin. You know how dangerous it is up here.' ... she said, 'I don't want to be dead. I want to come back. I miss you.' ... I said, 'Lisa, you can't come back. You're dead. You'll scare everyone. You just scared me.' ... and Richard, he also had a bad ep-leptic at school and that was that for Richard ... he came flyin up through the floor and took her but she quickly popped back and said, 'The one good thing is you don't need a telephone book down here.'

66

'... one night I woke up really suddenly in the dormitory cause on me Mind Screens I heard someone cryin ... I knew it was my Lisa so I leapt up those stairs quick as a skinny lizard and she was vomitin and sick on the floor and I rushed to the assistants but they wouldn't get up and so I went back and I picked her up and carried her to the chair and I kissed her and said, 'Goodbye darlin. Goodbye.' ... and I sang my song to her ... *a whale car knack, a whale car knack, ball bag on you paddle a whale he he, fly for nothin hey, fly for nothin hey, big mouth, small eyes, small cool lap, duck wag grill nah.*

'... the shunt in her head had got blocked ... in the mornin they rushed her to hospital but nothin they could do by then.

'... to tell you the truth Mum, sometimes I wanted to go there with my Lisa ... but I'm not thinkin along those lines no more now ... now I've got a real Mum and a real Dad and real bros, I mean bullas, and couses and a real home and I'm not just floatin free and I'm learnin pretty well quick smart again about being an Abadigenous Islander and so I'm not thinkin along those lines no more ... sorry about that, Mum, sorry about lettin down your atmosphere there.'

I'll wipe that.

'... hey Mum, this ull get ya laughin ... you say, 'Did you know Was-A-Boy was dead?' ... just say Was-A-Boy, but you can use anyone's name ... 'Did ya know Was-A-Boy was dead?' ... and you answer, 'Nah! Didn't even know he was in custody.' ... Kate hates me tellin that one ... doesn't get the joke ... always starts cryin like a real bloody gubba, hey Mum.

'... did ya hear that inflight ding? ... that's do up your safety belts for descent.

'... there's a couple of things I want to say to youse Mum ... firstly, I'm sorry to have missed you all these years Mum and

Dad but I didn't have your phone number ... I'm also sorry I don't remember your cookin but I'm really lookin forward to that big family feed-up La Cook-a-racha ... better late than on the never never ... I'm sorry Mum that you're a bit sick ... I'm sorry you got toes off from the Diabetics ... I'm really really sorry I couldn't speak to Dad the other night but now that I know his name I've decided to change from Warren to AAD—Albert-After-Dad—so I'm a real Islander now with a real Islander name ... Kate's not happy about it, as usual, says to wait and talk it over with my mother ... she is my mother ... she's really losin it Mum, if you know what I mean ... I'm a bit sorry you started to call her Mum, Mum, cause as far as I'm concerned, I've only got one mother who is you there in your hospital bed and that's that and I don't know how Kate's my Mum if she stole me ... as far as I'm concerned it's family if they help you and it's not family if they hurt you, end of story ... I'm sorry Kate says I can't come back and be an Islander with you and Dad and me bros and sisses and couses and that but if she doesn't let me I'm gunna tell that social worker Kate drinks all the time and smokes that yandi stuff and is one of those lesbian dykes and sleeps sex with women instead of men ... the sis who did my hair skull-ture said the Gubberment would let me come back and live with you because of all that and the TV program where I said about the slop-slop and the chicken coop ... I'm sorry I haven't got a better tape recorder to make a better tape quality for you ... I'm also sorry I haven't got all me CDs here with me ... Kate wouldn't let me bring em all ... I'm really sorry me little lady Rachael couldn't come up with me but Kate wouldn't buy her a ticket and I'm really mad about that ... anyway, I'm just sorry.

'... did you hear that Mum and Dad? ... we're about to touch down on home turf so I'm now in the same city as you and Kate's going to send this at the airport so I'll probably be arrivin at the same time as me voice on tape so I can just sit there and open and close me mouth while you play the tape … that'll make you laugh … that'll be just like me … keepin up the atmosphere … makin em laugh and makin em cry … in-personating meself, as usual.'

DELLKEITH

HOLY SUFFERING WHITEMAN
(English language title)

KOLERA TONAR
(Meriam Mer — Eastern Islands language title)

AUGADTH KIKIRIU MABAIG
(Kala Lagaw Ya — Western Islands language title)

TEN VERY GOOD REASONS

Look at the silly fool of a man out there. I swear he does it deliberately to annoy. But I'll have the last laugh old fella. You can bet next door will be taking great delight watching from the window. I can just hear her tomorrow. 'Oh we saw Keith 'pruning' those hibiscus bushes in his lovely frilly apron.' Look at him, such an old woman, placing them ever so in his basket. I know what you need, you need a good cold shower my man.

There! That's the watering done at least.

Je-sus-bloody-ch-rist-almighty! Calm man, stay calm, just continue as if nothing out of the ordinary's going on. Lalalal. 'Sweet vio-lets, sweeter than the rosies.' That bitch of a woman. She's mad, absolutely stark raving bonkers. Don't say a word, don't give her the satisfaction. Just go along to get along. Remember, it's her way or the highway. 'Knockey, knockey, knockey, will you please open the doorey dearie? Lemme in, lemme in or I'll huff and I'll puff and I'll blow the doorey in.'

How on earth? You fool of a man. It's not even raining. You're absolutely saturated. How on earth? No! Don't tell me. As if I haven't got enough to contend with. Kate's upsetting you before she even gets here. Typical! But you're more trouble nowadays than even Kate ever was.

1/—mischievous incontinency

Now get into that bathroom and take those wet clothes off. Kate and the boy will be here any minute.

No! No! Unhand me woman. Anything but that. Have mercy! I'm virginal. Without sin or stain.

Do I still have the oomph, Keithie-weithie?

Ah! serenade me Dillie-delly, my golden throated warbler and you'll have your answer.

'I'll be with you in apple blossom time
I'll be with you la la la'

Question here wifey dear! What do tiles and a woman have in common?

Loveliness that costs so little, loveliness that lasts so long?

No! Try again.

Whispered compliments at every turn of the head?

No! Answer? If you lay them right the first time you can walk all over them.

2/—sexual trampling

You just wait fella.

Another 'symptom' to scratch into that little black book of yours my dearest dear?

You'll keep. As you know, dearold Dr Clementine advised me to note down all the symptoms so he can make a thorough Diagnosis, Prognosis and Assessment. It's for your own and Katie's good, despite what you may think. *Complete Family Profile* he calls it. He only needs 10 Early Onset points in toto so I'll have oodles of leeway. Now stop dripping onto that W$\mathcal{ELC}$OM$\mathcal{E}$ mat and get into the bathroom. No! Wait! Don't you dare drip all over my freshly polished floor.

Ah! You wish me to fly to you my little mutton-dressed-as-lamb bird on magical wings of love. Flap flap

flap! Flap! Flap! Flaaap! Mayday! Mayday! Hoostan, we have a problem.

You're more trouble than you're worth. Here, step on this.

That's today's paper. You know I haven't read it yet.

Stand there all day then. It's up to you. I'll just kneel here and wait. I can wait all day if kneels be.

I've got ten good reasons myself. Ten reasons why a beer is better than a woman.

'shall we dance
on a bright cloud of music?
shall we fly?'

THE OLD FOLIE-A-DEUX TEN-STEP CAHOOTS CHORUS

One—a beer doesn't get jealous when you grab another beer.

Remember that first time, Keithie-weithie? My Broderie Anglaise bust cups.

Two—when you go to a bar you can always pick up a beer.

'I'll be with you
in apple blossom time'
**'her hair was soft
her eyes were blue
I knew just what she wanted to do.'**

Three—if you pour a beer right you'll always get good head.

'I'll be with you
to change your name to mine'

Four—you don't have to wash a beer before it tastes good.

'one day in May
I'll come and say'
I didn't know how but I tried my best
I started by placing my hand on her breast.
Five—a beer always goes down easy.
'happy the bride
that the sun shines on today'
Six—you can share a beer with your friends.
'what a wonder-ful
wedding there will be'
I remember my fear
my slow beating heart
how she slowly spread her legs apart.
Seven—beer is always wet.
'what a wonder-ful day
for you and me'
Eight—you always know you're the first one to pop a
beer.
'church bells will chime
you will be mine'
now when I did it I felt no shame
all at once the white stuff came
Nine—a frigid beer is a good beer.
'in apple—'
Ten—you can enjoy a beer all month long.
'—blossom time'
at last it's finished
it's all over now
my first time ever
milking a cow!
Aah! Made it. Ten steps to safety.

3/—wilful animalistic impotency

Don't you dare. Get out of that rotten stinking old chair and get into the bathroom. After you, that smelly old eyesore will be the next thing to go.

That on your list too?

I'm going into the bedroom to lay out dry clothes for you and you'd better be in that bathroom drying yourself when I get back or pity help you.

God created heaven and earth, then rested. God created man, then rested. God created woman and since then no bastard has rested. Why did god create beer? Answer! So that ugly old mutton birds could get laid.

I've laid out clean clothes, now get! Oomskey!

Everyone needs to believe in something. I believe I'll have another beer.

I'd advise you not to be difficult Keith.

When, with a little bit of effort, I can be bloody impossible Dellmay.

4/—disrespectful deliberate inebriated disobedience

Rule 1/—the boss is always right. Rule 2/—when the boss is wrong, refer to Rule 1.

It's all down here in my notebook.

Ditditdit, dotdotdot, ditditdit. I am coming into danger. Danger! Danger! You are coming into danger. Ditditdit, dotdotdot, ditditdit, dotdotdot.

NOTHING BUT A DISAPPOINTMENT

What nonsense have you got up to now?

Ah! Don't chuck em.

Hibiscus blooms make a marvellous display in situ on the bush—

Ah! They looked so pink and pretty.

—but wilt and die within hours when housebound.

I thought they'd make the lad feel at home.

He's blind, you fool.

5/—impromptu and unauthorised dead flower arranging

You silly looking thing! What is all this? Where did all this stuff come from? Ping-pong bats, Plastic Peggy doll with her head crushed in.

Didn't know I'd kep all her things, did you? They'll make the girl feel more at home. Ah! Don't chuck em. Keep looking. Don't avoid your ruby glass epergnes. There you go. Warm! Warm! Getting warmer! Really warm! Hot!

Rubber Ruby doll with her face scribbled out in biro, a paint-spattered 60s transistor radio. What next? Whatever next?

Cold! Cold! Getting colder!

Stupid mongrel! I should have known you were up to mischief when I heard you rummaging around in that disgraceful old shed of yours. That does it! A good spring cleaning's been on my wish-list for ages. As soon as Kate and Warren are dealt with, it's off to the tip with the lot. And you'll end up in something resembling one of these bin liners yourself unless you're very, very careful.

6/—hostile hoarding and aggravating home decorating

Keep looking. Don't avoid the *Encyclopædia Britannica*. Warm! Warm! Hot as hell. Our daughter made it herself with her own little hands, Dellmay. Look at that face, sewed real character into that. *Homunculus* she called it. Homunculus! An old black school stocking. What an imagination.

Ugh! ugly, disgusting, itchy thing it is. The stupid girl stuffed it with damned fibreglass from those old pink insulation batts. Ugh! One night I found her cuddling into it, 'for the comfort, Mummy,' she said, 'for the prickly-heat comfort.' Needless to say next day I chucked it while she was at school but, unbeknowns to me, brains trust here must have retrieved it—you fool of a man. 'Worse than a hairshirt, like sleeping with an old black Bogeyman,' I told dearolddoctor Clementine when he attempted diagnosis of the lunatic. Changeling. Artistic tendencies. Bad blood from bad paternal seed. Juvenile delinquency as soon as she turned teen. Yes, like sleeping with the Bogeyman. But this time the ugly thing's gone for good.

Aah! No, not that.

You've showed your hand this time, fella. All this lot, gone for good this time. And what have we here? Tucked in behind my Dresden China Crinolined Figurines—

She took to them like a duck to water. So bloody fem-a-nine. They remind me of her happy teenage years.

Happy teenage years! There were never any happy teenage years. Both of you, never anything but a disappointment. Her white, Sandler mini-heeled, Summer slingbacks I bought for her to wear with the A-line, popcorn pink stripey linen for her first afternoon date at the Interschool Boys' Rowing Regatta. But as soon as she could walk she ran, ran away from me. No! See! I can never get my tone right with her. She always makes me feel stupid somehow. I remember chasing her the length of the main street, twelve months pregnant with poordeardead Mark as I was. And like a little nasty devil she turned and laughed at me. Still, I always treated her as one of my own. A mother can't help that first surge of love no matter what she's got in her arms. It's hormonal, apparently. I never showed any favouritism between her and poordeardead Mark, despite her accusations. I've spent a lifetime making the home a haven.

I've spent a lifetime making the home a haven.

Mock away! Mock away! I won't give you the satisfaction of seeing you're upsetting me.

And I have other objectionable objects secreted about my person, if you'd care to frisk me, Mein Commandant. Voila! And from my breast pocket—zee vatch.

Not more rubbish. My god, that tarnished old watch. Cheap and nasty to begin with. I thought I'd seen the last of that years ago, too. Give it here! Come on, give it here!

I gave this to Kate when she turned sixteen but she didn't care.

DELLKEITH CAHOOTS CHORUS

She's never been anything but a disappointment.

Nothing but a disappointment. No! She didn't care.

Nah! Not her! Just chucked it in with her junk jewellery. Bought it for poor old Mum out of my first take-home pay when I was sixteen. Poor old soul, never had a thing in her life except the trouble us boys gave her and the heartbreak the old man dished out. I swore I'd never raise my hand to a woman.

But your hoof, ah, your hoof, now that was another anatomical matter altogether I suppose?

I've paid and I've paid. Dear god-in-heaven how I've paid.

And you'll go on paying if I have any say in the matter.

Poor old Mum. Couldn't get over my giving it to her. Kep it in the cheap little red velvet box it came in. Kep it on her dressing table on that white doily thing until the day she died, like it was the bloody crown jewels. She'd only ever wear it on special occasions. Wished I'd been a bit

**more bloody generous, bought the better one, when I saw
how much it meant to her.**

Ignorant bloody down-trodden bog Irish peasant out of
Armagh that she was.

**I always say she was the reason Women's Liberation
was invented. Came to this country starving, lice-ridden
and virtually illiterate during one of the perennial bloody
famines.**

Well, her housekeeping certainly left a lot to be desired.

**Yet she never seemed to stop acleanin and awashin and
so forth but it never seemed to make any difference, the
place was always mess enough to be ashamed of.**

And Kate's reverted to the same slovenly level of domesti-
city. I remember when she used to bring poor little Warren here
and he'd play on that very floor there with those little yellow
bulldozer Matchbox toys Kate bought for him. And I remember
saying to him once, out of her hearing of course, she's always
been so thin-skinned, I just knelt down beside the poor little
fellow and said, 'I bet you can't play like that on the floors she
keeps,' and he turned his big, sad, unfocused eyes on me and just
looked that sorrowful I could have cried. I just wanted to put
him out of his misery.

**Madam Sudden S-S-Smother Death is too
soft-hearted.**

That look of his said it all. But of course that was before
he got his hormones. I wouldn't like to get that close now. Any
reversion, she's inherited it. Like to like, eventually, I suppose.
Apparently sometimes it skips a generation.

**Poor old Mam. Sometimes she'd take a drop or two.
We'd go into the Ladies Lounge, 'the Snug' she'd call it.
They always put bowls of these tiny little biscuits on the**

tables in those days. I can still taste the damn things, sure I can as if me mouth were filled with them now. I'd sit there on the floor under the table playing with some little toy or other, eating those bloody dry little biscuits. I grew up on black tea brewed from yesterday's stewed leaves, stale bloody bread that had never seen butter, let alone jam, and those damned biscuits. Got bloody scurvy at one stage. Doctor had never seen a case before. And then the sighing would start and then the songs would start up, the brogue still on her.

'I'll take you home again Kathleen
to where your heart will feel no pain'

And I'd wait for the crying. Then she'd be patting and petting me.
'Me darlin' this and 'me darlin' that.

'and where the hills are fresh and green
I'll take you home Kathleen'

And she'd hold me to her and be telling me story after terrible story but in such deep Brogue, or some language I couldn't understand, that I couldn't fathom a word. But her face! Ah! her face, and the way it changed made it worse than if I could understand every damn word, and I'd say, 'in English Mam, in the English' and she'd stop, and I could tell she didn't know where she was and sometimes she wouldn't seem to know who I was for a minute.

'the roses all have left your cheek
I've watched them slowly fade and die'

And then she'd say, 'The niggers of Europe, love, that's what the rotten English bastards called us.' I can still hear her saying it as if she were sitting here beside me, 'The niggers of Europe, love, remember that at least.'

'your voice is sad when ere we meet
and tears bedim your loving eye'

'And in my vainglorious vanity I went and married one of the bastards. Och! No love! Not in the English. 'Tis better I carry all that I know to rot in the grave with me where t'will be dead, buried and silent, so you kiddies will never have to carry the burden of the shame. 'Tis just as that bone-useless rotter of a father of yours says, *Lest We Forget—The Solemn Ceremony of Silence. It's what makes this great country great.*'

Then she'd start up the wailing, like a bloody banshee, and the publican would throw us out into the back lane.

I think that calls for another toast, an icy one with a long, long cold neck. Ah! I've got just the ticket!

When I retired we went on one of those Qantas Fly-Drives back to the Mother Country, as Mein Furore insists on calling England. The package included a four-day Emerald Clover Over Tour of Ireland. I thought I might make some sense of those stories Mam told me but I'll tell you what, you can believe every derogatory bloody Irish joke you ever heard in your life. They're just that back-ward and pig-stupid. To an Irishman an enema is someone who's not your friend, a terminal illness is being sick at the airport, tumour means more than one and barium is what undertakers do. Everything they say about them is true—'The niggers of Europe' 's not too bloody far off the mark.

Snore on, you old fool. Softly, softly. Sneaky, sneaky. And—gotcha!

Bloody hell woman, you scared me half to death. Give it back. It's the only keepsake of Mum I've got left.

Cheap and nasty. You were a cheapskate even then.

Ah! Not that in the bin liner as well.

You'd have this place like a boong's midden heap given half a chance.

Now there's something you'd have some working knowledge of, if your s-s-smother's dying words are to be believed.

And if I were you, I'd remember, it **was** her death-bed.

7/—delusional black-and-blue-murder threatening

She always maintained you'd revert.

You dare! You dare! You've got nothing to revert to. You always were, always will be, your ignorant bogtrotter mother's bogtrotter son.

Temper temper. Remember your blood pressure.

Well, that's the tidying done. Now for the ironing. You just go back to your drunken fug you lazy, useless mongrel of a man.

'... oh Katie! Katie! ... I'm ironing the beautiful frock I made for your first day at university darling ... every frill and flounce and bow to perfection ... no one would ever have guessed what you were when I dressed you up all pretty in pink, darling ... like my very own little Dresden china doll ... I never meant it to get like this with you Kate, you're my only daughter ... it's supposed to be a special relationship by all accounts ... but somehow things just got worse and worse between us no matter what I tried … all the Specialists and Authorities I took you to—doctors, psychologists, phrenologists, psychiatrists, piano teachers, chiropractors, chiropodists, men of the cloth, sewing teachers, tennis coaches, June Dally-Watkins' School of Deportment and Beauty—and none of them wanted you either … never anything but a disappointment … and after a while there's no going back … when you have children of your own you'll understand why I've felt compelled to finally, with heavy heart in my breast, take the decisive actions I've been forced to take … with everybody's best interests at heart.'

With heavy heart in my breast. With everybody's best interests at heart.

'… I never know if I can safely introduce you around to the neighbours … never know what you'll come out with … never could keep a still civil tongue in your head … or how you'll be dressed … you've made me squirm I can tell you and, what's more, you seemed to enjoy doing it.'

For a while there she wouldn't even shave her legs. Remember that Keith? I thought I'd die of shame watching the neighbours and people at the shops smirk at each other and her big hairy legs in damn shorts no less. And no bra. All the years they treated me with the utmost deference and respect—the fruiter, the stationer, the pharmacist, the butcher. Never again have I been shown the same courtesy. Always a bit of a snide aside. Sometimes they asked after her, 'How's that young girl of yours, bright young thing,' they'd say. One day the stationer's wife took me aside and whispered with feigned concern, 'We heard she had to go to Sydney.' And even I didn't know a thing about it all. Still swears she's never had an abortion because she's, well, I'd be glad of even that rumour now. If they only knew the full extent—but I don't believe a word of it. Her father and poordeadbrother have always been lovely to her and a mother would know that sort of thing, she'd feel it. I can't bear her touching me knowing—well—knowing she touches other women like that. Ugh! Just the thought of it leaves a nasty taste in your mouth. Ugh!

Burr! Shudder! Burr! Something fishy there all right.

'... oh! Katie, it's as pretty a frock as I ever made you ... all the embroidered grubby roses snuggling in amongst the smocking and pintucking on the bodice ... I can't wait to see you in it again.'

No Keith, she **was** interested in boys I just don't know that they were too interested in her— the nonsense that came out of her mouth, the way she stooped. She seemed very keen on that lad who won the Cross Country that time. Kept that newspaper clipping about him hidden in the back of her diaries for years. How he'd been hit by a car, got up off the bitumen and not only finished the race, but won it, giving the police the number plate of the hit-and-run before collapsing. Now there's pluck! Could have done with a son-in-law like that around the place. I must remember to tell her how his marriage failed and he's divorced now. It's never too late.

And then there was the lad from the church group. Did I tell you, Keith, I saw his mother in the street the other day? He's gotten no better. I blame that damned university. Remember they'd never mention him and then he turns up out of the blue, dumb as a dog from some kind of drug overdose. She said he can't be left alone, they have to take him everywhere with them. She told me they'd just come back from a fishing trip and, hahaha, I shouldn't laugh, hahaha. She said they had to tie him to the car like a dog, hahahaha. I shouldn't laugh, it's terrible, hahahaha. But you can't help it can you? Imagine it. Brought her down a peg or two, she was always so hoity-toity. Always asked after Kate with a bit of a smirk. The laugh's on the other foot now. Tied to the car like a dog, hahahahah. I'm sure it's the kindest thing we could have done, to stop seeing them. They'd hate us to see them like that. I must remember to tell Katie, she'll be interested.

And just between me and myself, Keith's right about one thing, though I'd never give him the satisfaction of saying so, she did take to that first pair of white Sandler mini-heeled Summer slingbacks like a duck to water. I just don't believe it, you can't tell me she wasn't attracted to boys. I held her in my arms, I watched her grow up. She'd cry when she came home from functions because no one had asked her to dance. Now if that's not so very feminine—certainly not the way one of those sort of women behaves. She was always so demure, ladylike, a little piece of Dresden Blood and Bone china, the way June Dally-Watkins and I taught her a woman should be. But you have to laugh sometimes. When I asked her straight out if she hated men she said, 'No Dellmay!'—never called me Mummy—'it's just that I haven't found one who could cut the mustard.' Well, I have to agree with her there.

Look at him, snoring away, lying doggo.

Woof! Woof! Grur! Let sleeping dogs lie.

I've had to look forward to **that** coming home to me every night of my adult life. Street angel, home devil. Anyway I accepted her and her 'friend'. Sent her a Christmas card with **two** hankies last Yuletide. Two **women's** hankies instead of just the usual one. And not even an acknowledgment, not even a thank you came my way. It would kill her father if he ever even suspected.

It would kill her father if he ever even suspected.

Mock away all you like, your time's almost up mister. Though that's one thing I'll give the useless bloody fool, he always had staunch morals, walked away if anyone told a blue joke. Just didn't see the humour at that Silver Anniversary when they brought out the cake in the shape of a breast. We all roared but he went quite pale and had to sit down with his head between his legs when they plunged the knife in. I think people finally saw what I have to put up with and commiserated.

'... people know what you are too, Katie—wilful, arrogant, know-all, with the education your father and I paid for with the sweat-of-our-brow's-lifeblood ... it's a wonder you can walk up the street knowing that everyone knows what you are ... and then you, capableofanythingunderthesun, you go out, look for, and bring right back into the heart of the home, *Dellkeith*, the-home-which-is-a-haven-itself, all the misery, ugliness and filth of the world ... *Nulla-Nulla soap—knocks dirt on the head* as the old ad says ... well there always was something wrong there as dearolddoctor Clementine predicted ... I can still see him feeling the shape of your head, pointing out the bumps and bulges.'

Gee they're clever some of those authoritative old men. 'She'll never be quite right,' he said straight into my heartbreak. I can still see the clever look on his face.

DELLKEITH CAHOOTS CHORUS
'She'll never mature beyond the age of twelve—emotionally.'
I never told Keith.
I never told Keith.

8/—aggravating mirroring and mocking

Go on, keep it up, you're making it just that much easier for Dr Clementine and I to do the necessary. I've never told a living soul and I never will but I'm going to tell her this time round. Tell the truth and shame the devil and by gee some of those old slayings had a lot of philosophy in them. No! I'm too soft-hearted. I'll take that to the grave with me too.

I'm too soft-hearted.

Shame on both of you. She's never had to live with shame. I know what shame feels like. It's something you can't explain —shame. I never wanted any of my children to feel that and they never did. Kept the house clean and beautiful, you could eat off the floor. My motto has always been—Be Prepared for Royalty to Walk Through That Door. Never felt like the poor cousins. Treated like dirt we were.

Nulla-Nulla soap—knocks dirt on the head as the old ad says. But I learnt to hold my head high and stare them down in that rotten little sugarcane town. I vowed then and there that never again—I'd work and I'd scrimp and I'd save and never would I, or my children, ever have to feel what that shame felt like. Now she brings **him** right back into the heart of *Dellkeith* the-home-which-I've-worked-so-hard-to-make-a-haven. And she's not much better than the Blacks herself. My own flesh and blood. They say that's one good thing, no throwbacks, but I don't know if that applies to the Kanaka Race. They do say sometimes it skips a generation.

DELLKEITH CAHOOTS CHORUS
    never anything but a disappointment
    we built her a BBQ
    bought her a ping-pong table
    we turned on the string of coloured lights

every Saturday night
of her teenage generation-gap years
only to be made the butt of her bad-girl jokes
all those beautiful pure wool ensembles
I made for her
did I ever tell you
how I found them
all stuffed into a garbage bag
at the bottom of her wardrobe
full of rot and moth
like death
it was a s-s-smother's
love itself that died
then and there
the last straw that broke
the camel's back
I never tried again
and I buried it in the backyard
like a baby's body
still birth still birth still birth
still born still born still born
still borne still borne still borne

The doctors gave me Thalidomide. At least that's what I
told everyone when I lost the baby. One in five women bashed
while pregnant they said in the papers the other day, better odds
than the Pokies. I'm glad it died—nothing but a little crooked
wizened-up black ball of hair and teeth. And now she brings it
back into the home-which-is-a-haven.

I've paid and I've paid and I've paid. I've never stopped
paying and paying and paying.

CAHOOTS CHORUS CONTINUES
> **good money after bad**
> for her to be taught
> grooming and deportment
> by Miss June Dally-Watkins
> piano and singing
> by the Misses Skyrings
> **and we waited**
> **for the Saturday night sing-a-longs**
> **and the impromptu ping-pong challenges**
> **to start**
> waited for the young men
> to come calling
> with sheet music under their arm
> **despite our long-term, heart-felt**
> **investment**
> nothing but disappointment

**She's a bum, our only daughter's nothing but a bludger
and a bum.**

A FEW HOME TRUTHS
9/—dreadful daughter disparagement
> **Write this down in your little black book Madam
> Suddendeath-by-S-S-Smothering. I cannot see. I cannot
> pee. I cannot chew. I cannot screw.**
> Slower! Slower! I can't keep up.
> **My memory shrinks. My hearing stinks. No sense of
> smell. I look like hell. My body's drooping. Got trouble
> pooping. The golden years have come at last. The golden
> years can kiss my arse.**

Ah! blow it, I'll just write,

20+ — verbalbloodydiaorrhoea

You know you're going the same way as Mum did in the end—messing in the house, incontinent, won't let sleeping dogs lie buried, raking up a dead past better left undisturbed in unhallowed ground. Things that any decent, right-minded person would take to the grave with them for the sake of the sacred family name of poordeardeadbabyMark's poorlittleunborn children.

DELLKEITH CAHOOTS CHORUS
Lest We Forget
the Sacred Ceremony of abittabloody shush
s-s-smother mother—mum Mum, she's mum alright
hahaha
hahaha

Must have been the uncivilised pagan in Mum coming up. They all revert, eventually, unless every effort is made. I put-her-out-of-her-misery—eventually—and you'll be put out of yours unless you're very, very careful, my man. Why should any living soul, who has made every effort, put up with your form of nonsense?

God grant me the serenity to accept the things I cannot change, the courage to change the things I can and the wisdom-of-wifey to hide the bodies of those old birds I've had to knock off their perch because they started to squawk. Squawk! Squawk! Squawk! As our bald old galah used to say, 'If I had one more bloody feather I'd fly.' Squawk! Squawk! Squawk!

No! As dearolddoctor Clementine said on the day, and in your hearing, 'It was sheer kindness for sudden death to put her out of her misery.'

DELLKEITH CAHOOTS CHORUS
she didn't feel a thing
the bedclothes weren't even rumpled
the angels just came down
and did the merciful

One angel called Phenobarb, another called Asphyxia, singing that all-time, old-time favourite, 'Stay in Your Own Backyard'.

'go out and play as much as you may
but stay in your own backyard
what do you suppose they're going to give
a black little coon like you?'

There's no way in the world that dirty old Uncle Tommy Tanna was Mum's brother. Fair as fair. It was Mum's mind wandering. Good thing I put a stop to it wandering too far.
Good thing I put a stop to it wandering too far.
No! That's one thing, those Kanakas, they kept to themselves. We always just called him old Uncle Tommy, old Uncle Tommy Tanna, everyone did, out of respect for his age, I suppose. No, it was the black Irish in Mum, those looks. And I've always had a horror of the sun. Mum never let me out of the house without a hat on. And she explained why Aunty Iris let Dad in, but not her and us kids, that Christmas. Mum said there were too many for the table so we ate under the trees. It was nicer there anyway.

And those two little angels just kep on warbling.

'stay on top of your high board fence
but honey don't you cry so hard
what do you suppose they're going to give
a black little coon like you?'

You know Keith, when I look at you, you know what I think, I always think how sad it is to see someone as old and ugly and stupid looking so pleased with themselves.

'what do you suppose they're going to giiiivvvve
a blaaaack little coooon like yoooouuu?'

Lalala! I'm ignoring you in case you hadn't noticed. Lalala! I don't hear a thing. Lalala! And that was the last time we went to Aunty Iris's. Hardly acknowledged each other in the street after that. And those funny, 'You from Gin-gin my girl?' jokes Dad made to Mum and she'd blush and giggle. 'Horseplay,' Dad would say to us kids, 'just horseplay, kids.' They always made me squirm inside, those jokes of his. Anyway I'll take it all to the grave with me. Any hint of—Kate will never have to bear even the hint of a stain. Although she's shameless as—and roaming around in her hairy legs with that sick boy. I told her then and no she wouldn't listen, I said—

DELLKEITH CHANT THEIR I-TOLD-YOU-SO-AT-THE-TIME CAHOOTS CHORUS
don't you remember
we said to you twelve years ago Kate
we said

he's a novelty now
but in a few years
it'll be a different story
don't you think it would be kinder
to leave him where he is
so he doesn't get used to another way
because when you return him
as you undoubtedly will
you've never stuck to anything in your life
it will be all that more terrible for him
knowing what he's missing
you'll rue the day
a rod for your back
don't say we didn't warn you
don't ever say
we didn't say
we told you so
at the time

It's 5:30 and I haven't even done the dusting or set the table. She's already put my whole day out of kilter before she's even arrived. And if she thinks he's going to eat off my good Shelley Blood and Bone she's got quite another think coming. Those chipped old Bunnykins from when she was a naughty Fail-to-Thrive baby will do for him. He wouldn't notice the difference anyway. And I'll make the couch up for him on the back verandah, where he belongs, just in case. The best laid plans can always still go awry. You don't want Darkies inside the house, especially after dark. I know I wouldn't sleep a wink from worry.

DELLKEITH'S 6 PM RSL APOLOGIA

On your feet woman. Show some respect. Raise your right paw in salute and say after me—Lest We Forget. The Spirit of Ozzie-ozzie-ozzie Oy-oy-oy. The Solemn Ceremony of a-bit-a-bloody-shush, a-bit-a-bloody-mum's-the-word, is what makes this great I-still-call-Australia-home country great. Mozzie-mozzie-mozzie scratch scratch scratch. I'm sorry. I'm so very sorry that so many of us died stopping the slit-eyed Nips from liberating the indigenous peoples of Australia. I'm sorry that we came to this continent, when it would have been so much better to leave it to the dyke-digging Dutch or the frog-friggin French or those plonk-plastered Papist Portuguese who had such enlightened colonialisationist policies. I'm sorry that decent middle-class families committed wholesale a-similar-relationsist gendercide, that is, adopted Black kiddies as their own rather than spend their money on overseas holidays or new household appliances and leave the children to die of syphilis and leprosy and petrol-bloody-sniffing in some outback hovel somewhere. I'm sorry that misguided jurists tried to introduce justice and fair play to that amazingly advanced tribal law system that entitles someone to rape and murder the sister of anyone that may offer offence. That we put Black people in custody when all they ever did was murder, rape, assault, sell drugs, starve their children, urinate in public, dob on us to the United Nations, murder our sheep and cattle and horses and dogs and chooks and daughters and wives—well, they can't be all bad.

I'm sorry that we always precisely pinpoint sacred sites on which to undertake mining. I'm sorry that a pile of bloody rocks and a few stories about turtles doesn't

95

constitute land-bloody-tenure in any civilised legal system that I know of. I'm sorry that we embarked on culturally autocratic policies like childhood immunisations, free milk, free housing, free medical care, free education, free sniffing-petrol, free airfares. Sorry that eight hundred million dollars or thereabouts is insufficient to maintain the Volvo-driving Black bureaucracy, or maintain three free four-wheel drive vehicles per indigenous humpie per boong per grog-soaked year. I'm sorry that we are so patronising as to reserve university places for indigenous people who don't even pass primary school, and reserve public service places and police force places and local government places and arts council places and I'm sorry for having the temerity to realise that every Black in a monkey suit I see on TV is a tokenistic, on-welfare-handouts recipient receiving an honorary degree from a university that I never even heard of and never had a hope in hell of getting into myself in the first place. And the thing I'm most most altogether and heart-feltly sorry about is that we dared to elect a Prime Minister who won't apologise for something we never did and if we did we'd do it again because we were flamin well right to do it in the first place.

I'm sorry we imposed The Golden Rule—Those Who Got the Gold Make The Rules. I'm sorry. I'm sorry. I'm sorry. Bejesus you can see how flamin apologetic I can be when pushed so don't push me much bloody further.

Well, Keith, I'll tell you what I regret. I regret we bred a mad daughter who has seen fit to go her own wicked way and drag that poor little scrap of a lad around with her when any thinking, feeling person would know he was better off in Care for his, and everybody else's, protection. But that's to be rectified directly.

I regret the years I spent working hard, living right and trying to do the right thing. I regret whatever went wrong between us so we never could be friends, talk the way parents and children should, as seen on TV. I regret that, as per constabulary advice, I've had to inform the Authorities about the irregularities of the situation and this unauthorised reconciliation across State lines. Did I tell you Keith that that police sergeant I spoke to was on the parochial council with you? Did I tell you how concerned and helpful he was? Did I tell you that he said we had every right to be concerned? Did I tell you that he inquired as to whether I'd viewed that film— *The Chant of the Blacksmith*? Did I tell you he said it was proof that our fears are quite legitimate? Did I tell you he said that anything can send them off—a red rag, the smell of alcohol, a wrong word in the wrong ear, a full moon, no moon, too much noise, too much silence, anything? Did I tell you that he said that, until we sorted things out, he'd get the van to drive past on a regular basis with its light flashing to make its presence felt? Did I tell you he was genuinely worried about the situation? Did I tell you he said he had daughters of his own and he felt sad for us to think that our own flesh and blood, a creature we'd brought into the world, was thoughtless enough to be putting us in this situation? Did I tell you he said I could ring him any time, day or night? Did I tell you he gave me his mobile number? Did I tell you he said that, from the letter, which I read out to him, and he's studied Psychology at the Academy, did I tell you he said, in his considered opinion, she sounded as if she wasn't quite right, wasn't coping, was crying out for help? And did I tell you he said that sometimes you've got to be cruel to be kind—the technical terms for it, apparently, are *tough love* and *zero tolerance*—and that that unenviable task usually falls to the parent? Did I tell you he said perhaps we should consider taking the facts of the case to a higher, more relevant Authority? Did I tell you he asked if the Department of Children's Services knew, for instance? Did I tell you I did contact the Department? Did I tell you that that same lovely Tiffany, who did all she could to help us stymie the paperwork and nip this fostering nonsense in the bud all those years ago, is Head of the Department now? No, I make no apology for the fact that yes, I have sought advice from the Children's Services Department. Did I tell you I said to her, here we both are, all these years later, still trying to sort out Kate's mess? She was just that grateful to me for sending her Dr Clementine's original Diagnosis, Prognosis and Assessment of Kate and I enclosed a copy of that bleat of a letter Kate sent us for good measure. Did I tell you how horrified Tiffany was when I told her about Kate's sexual orientation and the mess of her mental history? She had no idea about what the boy's been up to—all his going walkabout and so forth. Apparently the Protection Act that most of them were kept under has, unfortunately, been abolished, and so it's been proving a bit hard for the Authorities to rope him in. Kate's been frustrating all attempts as could be expected. But Tiffany said that this time Kate'd be well and truly kiboshed. Did I tell you she said this is 'Unauthorised and Unsupervised Reconciliation Across State Lines'? Tiffany was so concerned that she's going to come here herself, personally, with her Crisis Management Team and collect the boy. Did I tell you all I have to do is ring her as soon as he gets here? And did I tell you that when I told dearolddoctor Clementine the full extent he was shocked and said that the Authorities don't let women like that anywhere near children even in this permissive day and age? And did I tell you how the dearoldfellow had the decency not to rub it in, not to say I-told-you-so-oh-so-many-years-ago-that-it-would-come-to-this eventually? No, you see, I'm all empathy. I could read it there in his face as clear as if I was reading that newspaper. I'm all empathy.

You're all empathy.

He said this time he'd sign the Papers for her to get the help she so urgently needs. All I have to do is ring him when she gets here.

Ditditdit! Dotdotdot! Ditditdit! Danger! Danger! You are coming into danger! Ditditdit! Dotdotdot!

DELLKEITH CAHOOTS CHORUS
give us a wink
give us a nod
in the same boat
peas in a pod
shoulder to shoulder
hand in glove
pull together
stand together
club together
hang together
hold together
live together
die together
combine our force
endorse, endorse
in league with the devil
hunting in couples

That poor little scrap of a lad was lucky enough to get away from those Blacks. He should be grateful for that, not rushing to get back to them. And Kate, the fool of a girl, actually encouraging this ridiculous and, apparently, even dangerous, *unauthorised and unsupervised reconciliation across State lines*. She says here in this letter she's afraid the Authorities will find out. At least she has some inkling of how wrong what she's doing is. This Stolen Generation nonsense—

CAHOOTS CHORUS—GLEE CLUB 1
ha ha ha
ha ha ha
whatever that is when it's at home
whatever that is when it's at home

has seen her go from 'a Christian Goody-Two-Shoes' to a 'Genocidal Assimilationist Colluding with a Racist Regime'.

CAHOOTS CHORUS—GLEE CLUB 2
ha ha ha
ha ha ha
what on earth's this nation coming to?
what on earth's this nation coming to?

And what's she trying to prove? That's what I want to know. She doesn't fool anyone running around with that sick lad in tow. People know what she is. He was a cocky with a clipped wing. Couldn't run from her like everyone else.

CAHOOTS CHORUS—GLEE CLUB 3
ha ha haha
ha ha ha
until now

until now

Yes! Until now. Subnormal as he is, even he's seen through her.

CAHOOTS CHORUS—ANTIPHON 1

He's not the total fool he looks.

Everyone eventually sees through her. And apparently that TV program we saw him on has stirred things up. Telling everyone she kept him in a chicken coop down the back and fed him slops in a bowl like a dog. Telling everyone how she stole him from his tribe. She says here in this bleat of a letter she's *got to be brutal enough to tell him the truth.*

She shouldn't have any trouble on that score.

Well now she might get a taste of the pain of the stain of shame. Let's see how she likes it. And the boy's apparently going Walkabout all the time as his hormones kick in and he regresses. See how she likes sitting up by the phone night after night, ringing the hospitals, the police, the morgue like we had to with her and her shenanigans.

She says here that she needs our help. Do you, don't you think we ought to—?

That's what the Authorities are there for.

Ditditdit! Dotdotdot! Ditditdit! Ditditdit dotdotdot ditditdit.

SHOCK JOCKS ON VOX POP

That's one thing I agree with the Black radicals on Johnronallenstan—like should stick to like. A place for everything and everything in its place. As my dearoldaunty Iris used to say, 'You can't go against Mother Nature.'

You can't turn on the wireless or the television set nowadays without seeing bloody Blacks whingeing. As John Elliott so rightly says, 'We're the laughing stock of the civilised world. Who's ever heard of a conquering nation, after over two hundred years, giving back what it's won, to those who it bloody well won it from?' It's just bad sportsmanship, Dellmay, bad business practice all round.

As you always say, Johnronallenstan, 'It was a war—'

A bitasense from a female at last. Yes Dellmay, correct. Survival of the bravest, fittest, strongest, smartest, whitest.

And we won, didn't we Jonronallanstan? End of story.

Indeed we did Dellmay. Sad, but a scientifically proven fact, we won. End of story.

All this care and consideration for Warren's so-called Natural Mother, for a woman who neglected and abandoned, bashed and abused him and none at all for her own parents who— Did we ever?

DELLKEITH CAHOOTS CHORUS
hardly ever

I'll admit
I could be a bit quick
with my fists
and true
I've had occasion
to be swift with a kick
but remember how she provoked

Sorry listeners for that dead air there. But here's another request from a lovely lady out there. Another all-time,

low-down fab fave from those mop-top scallywags. A toon of the footatappin, karaoke-inducin, singalongwithme sort, 'Michelle Ma Belle'. Lala lala lalalalallalalalallla lalala.

Trust you to bring that up. I was provoked beyond human endurance as well you know. Wouldn't even give a rendition of that lovely ballad for the Parochial Council Ladies Auxiliary Afternoon Tea. Not on your life, not her. Snuck up the back steps—late. My fingers just itched I can tell you, as any mother's would, when I saw her slinking past the lounge like that. And after I'd specifically requested her presence. Always a mistake to ask anything of her. Intent on making a show of me in front of those ladies who were all so refined, so carefully and beautifully turned out. I'd done everything—cooked two different types of shortbread, three different Anglican Slices topped with desiccated coconut and a strawberry Victoria sponge served up on my best Shelley and Mum's silver tea service. The only lovely thing the pooroldsoul ever owned or could hand me down. Well, Kate will never get her hands on it I know that much. I've stipulated that Legally and Officially in my Last Will and Testimony to her arrogance. And she stood there in her impeccably laundered Grammar School uniform in which she could have looked so very nice if she'd only held herself properly. She looked at me with that ugly, freckled, accusatory, tight-lipped, clench-jawed frightened face that I'm sure she practised in the mirror for just such important well-me-I'm-only-her-mother occasions and she put down her Globite and her gold-initialled music case and she stomped in. 'Heiling' me with her raised fist. I thought I'd die of embarrassment. One lady giggled and another spilt her Twinings English Breakfast on her Sportscraft tartan. 'Heil!' Whatever that means. Showing off the French we were silly enough to have her taught I suppose.

And she stomped across the Axminster—we couldn't afford Westminster in those days—and lifted the lid of the Steinway Upstanding and thumped. It's an ugly word but the truth will out. A girl who'd been given all the attributes and trained in all the refinements. She thumped out, at break-neck, break-neck speed, the most dreadful rendition of 'Michelle Ma Belle' as is humanly possible. And then she stomped out. Nobody knew where to look or what to say. One lady had to excuse herself with a fit of the giggles. My lovely afternoon ended awkwardly and abruptly. Pro-voked be-yond hu-man en-dur-ance. Oh! Oh! Oh!

Oh? Oh? Oh?

I never laid a hand on her!

Ha ha ha ha.

Now stop right there Keith. If the truth be told—She. Bashed. Me.

Ha ha ha. You're a riot.

DELLKEITH CAHOOTS CHORUS

you've got to admit
I'm the first to admit
I'm not always right
well I'm white alright
white with anger
she always was
a soft touch
for any lame-duck
lost-dog
that cared to limp in
off the street but
the backyard's still full

of those dead birds
and lizards
and fruit bats
she'd wrap
in my best white linen
hankies
with hand-crocheted borders
and bury them
under paddle-pop stick
crosses
in her pet cemetery
but—
carried
the worries of the world
on her back
but—
she's bitten off
she's bitten off
she's bitten off
more than she can chewy, chew, chew
with this latest lot
so boo hoo hoo
oh boo hoo hoo
now all her chickens
are coming home
to roost
in the coop
she's built
for herself
too boo hoo hoo
oh too too boo hoo hoo

Aw! Ha ha ha. **Stop woman, stop! You're breaking my heart. Ha ha ha.**

Crocodile tears.

TELL THE TRUTH AND SHAME THE DEVIL

And old Uncle Tommy Tanna from next door, lured me into the sugarcane that day. Promised me one of those little dollies he made from cow hair he collected from the barbed-wire fences around the place. Ingenious little plaited things with arms and legs and faces. Put them in the trees to lure parrots for his parrot curries. Always promised me he'd make a really pretty one for me when I grew up. Thought I must have been grown up that day when he lured me into the sugarcane. One in three little girls apparently, if the newspapers are to be believed. Dad would have killed him if he'd ever found out, I knew that, so I never breathed a word to anyone. It's something I'll take to the grave with me. 'My little white lubra,' he whispered, 'pale as day but blow me yellow satin still bangs like black velvet when you get down to the purple pussy.' I haven't thought of those words for years but now, with Kate bringing him back into the house, old Uncle Tommy's words just keep playing over and over in my mind. Now I can't get those words out of my head—again.

I've spent all my life just hanging on. And the exhaustion—that's what none of you understands. You laugh at me when I nod off as soon as I flop in front of the tele. I know I can be hard, sharp with my tongue and quick with my fists. A bit slaphappy at times, I suppose.

'… but every time, before I see you Katie, all your life really, I've thought **this** time, when you come home from school, from holidays, from hospital … this time a mother will sit down with her only daughter and really open up ... we'll really talk ... perhaps some form of apology's in order ... woman to woman ... but an apology cuts both ways, you know' ... I know what I'm going to say too, I've rehearsed it for years now ... I'll start with, 'I know I've been a bit hard over the years but the statistics don't lie Kate.' ... and she'll laugh at the lameness, I can hear her now ... and then the accusations and counter-accusations will start ... I can hear it now ... and I'll be forced to tell the truth and shame the devil, as they say ... but it needs to be said ... No Kate, I'm sick and tired of all your lies, of keeping quiet to protect you from yourself. The truth is, Kate—You. Bashed. Me.'

Give it a bloody rest, woman.

Go ahead, laugh, the laugh will be on the other side of your face once dearolddoctor Clementine gets hold of this documentation. The thing you don't understand, none of you has ever understood or given—no. See. I nag. I should just satisfy myself with saying, quite simply, I'm Frozen Inside—and leave it at that.

And now, listeners, a spot a kulcha of the poetical persuasion befitink the ockasion.

when things go wrong as they sometimes will
when the road you're trudging seems all uphill
when the funds are low and the debts are high
and you need to smile but you have to cry
when care is pressing you down a bit
don't complain to me
I don't give a shit

20 something going on 30+/— livelong lifelong apathy

I know you won't believe me but I wasn't always like this.
Once I was Young and Lovely and full of Happy Hope and all
I wanted was a Handsome and Kind Husband and a Handsome
and Kind Son who'd become a Doctor and a Pretty Little Girl
I could Dress Up and Show Off and who'd Marry a Handsome
and Kind Medical Doctor. Now can anyone tell me what's so
wrong with that? And look at what I've ended up with.

**Ditditdit dotdotdot ditditdit. To be sure, to be sure, to
be sure another long-neck seems perfectly in order for a
condemned man.**

'... when I had you Katie my first thought, when I looked
down at your little delicate fingers curling around my finger—'

At your little delicate fingers curling around my finger—

'... I thought *a friend for life* and I loved you so much ...
you'll never know, with no children of your own, the way a
mother' ... but I should have taken the *r* out of friend.

But I should have taken the r out of friend.

I had a fiend for life.

DELLKEITH CAHOOTS CHORUS—ANTIPHON 2
you'll never know the love
a mother
the love
a father
but that dream was short-lived
as soon as you could talk you said 'no'
just turned your ugly-as-sin-itself little face
to the wall and said
'no no no no no no'
as soon as you could walk
you just ran

ran away from me
and the way that she clenched
those delicate little hands
into fists
even in her sleep
hanging on to something
in grim life
for grim life
and it's that same wilful stubbornness now
still hanging on to her anger
still hanging on to that boy
it's sheer wilful anger
keeps her clinging
onto that sinking ship of a lad
she says in her letter that he's suicidal
well
honestly
who isn't
you just have to grin
and bear it
and living in her usual
fantasyland
about the abilities of that boy
but
looking at this photo she enclosed
I swear he's looking whiter
well they do say environment helps

I want to say to her, talk like a mother, ... Katie, oh Katie!
darling! I'll never understand you, never, never, never ... and I'd
give anything in the world—

I want to say to her, talk like a father, 'Ever felt, late at night Kate, ever felt lonely and lost and wondered what you were doing with him, wasting all your God-given talents on a subnormal like him? Hiding your light under a barrel and he's the barrel? Ever felt that?' I plan to say to her, 'I know I don't need to tell you this Kate, but there's always your little pink bedroom lying in wait for you here, just as you left it, if ever you—well, you know what I'm trying to say so let's just leave it at that.'

That's if they let us take her for home visits, Keith. Dearolddoctor Clementine says we can't know that for sure until after the Authorities carry out their Diagnosis, Prognosis, Assessment and Case Plan. He's already set the wheels in motion from his end. Now it's up to us to follow through. It's indicative that she thinks she knows better than the Authorities regarding Warren. Knows better than all the Doctors, Optometrists, Ophthalmologists, Neurologists, Social Workers, Psychologists. It was there in black and white, *black, blind and profoundly retarded*. She showed me. No school would take him. So she leaves the State with him, gives up her job and teaches him herself. Even his own didn't want him. If even your own mother doesn't want you—those Islanders know how to look after themselves.

I can vouch for that. I saw it all when I was up there in '44–'45. Subsistence economy—gardeners and fishermen. Looked after their own. I know more than she thinks I know about him and his so-called 'people'. Thought they were mates. I don't mind saying I loved those blokes. I thought we were mates until I realised they'd thrown the whole damn crop of wongai berry into the sea so we wouldn't eat them. Didn't understand the significance at first but then I heard that they reckon if you eat the fruit of the wongai you'll come back to the Islands. When I realised they'd chucked away the whole year's crop, every fruit they could find, well that put a bit of a different bloody complexion on things from thereonin with me. Thursday Island, huh! Broken Bottle Island we called it. And V-bloody-D was so prevalent up there we called it the old T. I. handshake.

We all have a duty to civilise but you can take it too far. Charity begins at—sometimes I'm sure I do feel things more deeply than others. Sometimes, when we'd drive down along the river there and pass that Cherrymead I'd see those poor little scraps of kiddies in the yard wandering around aimlessly with their blank faces and dribbling mouths, grunting and moaning. I'm sure I do feel things more deeply than others, I'd pray that the river would just rise up one day and take them all away. And you know Keith, I couldn't help but wonder what kind of a person Kate was to work there all that time and then actually foster that sick, sick lad. Actually take it home with her. No, I'm sure I do feel things more deeply than most people. I'm all empathy.

You're all empathy.

A MOTHER'S LAMENT AND A WIFE'S ACCUSATION

I'll say to her, 'Do you have any idea what it's like just holding on, inside, waiting until it's better and it never is, never does get any better.' I've accepted that now but the habit of holding on's still there and it's stood me in good stead really, more discipline, and get more done in a day, than everyone else combined. Just look at Keith there for instance, does half a day's work and then on his fat backside with a beer. I'd have been perfectly happy—I know I'm hard—but I would have been perfectly happy to see Kate and Warren stay at a hotel but, for reasons known only to himself, he decides to put his hoof down for the second time in his pathetic life. Still birth, still birth, still birth.

Will you ever stop making me pay and pay and pay?

That's where she got it from, from you, you mongrel. Time and again I've seen that same flaming look flare up in her eye. There I go—swearing. She's the only person in the world who can reduce me to verbal filth and she hasn't even set hoof in the house yet. Even as a baby, that look in her eye, challenging me, defying me. That's when I knew dearolddoctor Clementine's predictions were accurate. I've got nothing on my conscience but attempts. No one would have guessed, when I dressed her up all pretty-in-pink. Still trying all those years on. Hanging on to the hope she'd come good. Even this beautiful frock I slaved over for months for her to wear for her first day at university. All those grubby little roses. All those tiny little bright pink patches of knotted silkthread. All the little bits of miscarriage I had to pick out of my panties that night, last time you put your hoof down.

If I'd confessed I'd have been tried, jailed and released years ago.

Still birth, still birth, still birth. Spreading. Spreading.

Jesus! Here we bloody well go again.

All the clotted and caked rags I found in Mum's bedside table. I never said a word. The solemn ceremony of Mum's-the-word. Just waited for years for her to die of the Cancer. Until I found out it was only her periods. That's how innocent. Needle pricking into—Hoof kicking into—One in five—Pricking into—Like cockroach eggs and the hundreds of baby cockroaches scattering. When I dressed her up pretty as a prettylittle little Shelley Blood and Bone china figurine she was. Just look at the photo of the three of us in Ye Olde Worlde World's Living History Village that Australia Day that we gave her this silver locket for her thirteenth, Keith. Mum gave it to me for my thirteenth with one of my little baby curls inside. Needless to say Kate just chucked it in with all her junk jewellery when she got home. I retrieved it and kept it on the sideboard with this keepsake photo. How debonair you'd have looked as an English officer rigged out in your Red Coat like that and Katie and I in pink poplin crinolines and matching bonnets. See, there's Katie wearing the locket. I even plaited locks of all our hair, deardead Mark's included, and entwined them together forever inside. But she didn't care. Just in with her junk jewellery when she got home. Never anything but a disappointment despite all my efforts. As God and this photograph are my witnesses, before God and the camera, I tried. I've got nothing on my conscience but attempts. Mark would have been such a lovely, obedient sweet little thing. I could have just loved and loved him. He couldn't get enough of his Mummy. To this day that's what he'd have called me—'Mummy'—I'm sure of it. Sometimes, when I sit quietly sipping Twinings from my matching floral Shelley Blood and Bone cup, saucer and plate set from my mirror-backed, pink plush upholstered china cabinet, pouring tea from Mum's EPNS teapot delicately embellished with its intricate pattern of roses and strawberries, the embroidered linen tablecloth with crocheted edging and corners I worked by the light of a kerosene lamp, for my Glory Box all those years ago, sitting here at my round, French polished, rosewood table with the Bohemia-cut crystal basket full of golden plastic wheat stalks centrepiece, surrounded by my what-nots and shadow-boxes full of Shelley and Dalton and Wedgwood and Dresden, all my lovely historically-accurate-down-to-the-smallest-detail figurines and silver-framed family photos, my poor sore corned and carbuncled feet comfy and secure on the floral

Westminster, I swear when I shut my eyes I can hear the word 'Mummy' in the mouth of a little boy. 'Ma-me, Ma-me, Ma-me.' See, there he goes, cooing away. So there's no way I'll accept that I'm a failure as a mother.

DELLKEITH CAHOOTS CHORUS
    she never called me mummy
    she never called me daddy
    always Dilly-dellie this
    and Keithie-weithie that
    or Dellkeith so and so

All brass. Never a hint of respect. So let them stay in a hotel, that's what I say. If she can't even call me 'Mummy', 'Mummy's' a sacred word, then she's no daughter of mine. And the cheek, the nerve—Last time they were here, oh yes, she'd let him call me 'Grand-ma'. Just to annoy. She's got a genius for that. Turned my stomach when that little Black face looked up and used that word. Brrr! Still chills. All the wizened-up filth and mess of the world brought home to roost right in the heart of *Dellkeith*, to a name she used to make light of and s-s-nigger at. Making a damn mockery. And, to tell you the truth, I wouldn't be surprised if that wasn't her whole and sole motivation for taking him on in the first place and her stubbornness in sticking with him despite all the trouble and misery he's causing her. **He** even wants to get away from her. And now that all her chickens are well and truly coming home to roost, she comes back to *Dellkeith*, limping for sympathy.

    I saw enough of that when I worked for OPAL, that One Person of Australia League, that time. Spent months trying to show those women out at Darra Housing Commission how to economise, like I had to for so many years myself. Showed them what you could do with a cheap cut of meat or a pound of sausage mince. And what did I get for my troubles—never so much as a thank you. You can't just thumb your nose for years at everything society and the family holds dear, smash everything they hold sacred, and then think you can just waltz back into the sanctity and ask for protection. After you've burnt all your bridges there's no way to get back across that river. It's just sheer brass on her part that she thinks she can just lob in and bludge off us after all these years.

DELLKEITH CAHOOTS CHORUS—ANTIPHON 3
> **it can't be done**
> totally unreasonable
> **all a parent wants is to protect**
> but she never allowed us that privilege
> **insisted on learning the school-of-hard-knocks way**
> well let her learn then
> **let the higher education begin**
> **let 'The Sin(ce) of the Past' roll past**

DELLKEITH AND THE 'AVC' SING 'THE SIN(CE) OF THE PAST'
> *in that dust on the table*
> *in that dirt on the floor*
> *'we do not disappear into thin earth*
> *we are thin earth,'* sang the Terra Firma
> *in the ash in the air*
> *in the bones on the beach*
> *'we do not disappear into thin air*
> *we are thin air,'* sang the Holy Smoke

That'll be them now. That's a taxi just turning into the street. Ditditdit. Dotdotdot.

They're here then. I've got to get to the phone.

There's a mob of Blacks living between the gloss finish exterior Dulux enamel and the Taubmans interior satin finish of our walls. What do they want?

There's a mob of Blacks living in the dark under our sanded and Estapoled floorboards. Why are they there?

There's a mob of Blacks living between our Miracoil mattress and our bed springs. What are they waiting for?

There are Black voices between the stations on our radio. What are they saying? Just out of earshot.

There are Black faces flickering in the static between our TV channels. What do they want?

There are Black voices whispering in the white noise between the tracks on our CD. What are they trying to say, just out of earshot?

Dirt poor we were. Dirt floor. Mum swept and wet and tamped it down with her bare feet every day. Hessian bags walls. Hessian bags stretched on saplings hammered into the dirt floor for beds. Hessian bags full of newspaper for blankets. Washing the clothes Persil-white at night crouched down in the irrigation ditch to hide my shame. Lived no better than the Blacks in those days. Treated like dirt. Nothing but shame.

Dirt floor. Dirt poor. Dirt road. Dirt cheap. Dirty work. Dirty trick. Dirty money. Dirty dog. Hit me. Hit me. You dirty dog you bit me. Dirty look. Dirty linen. Eat dirt. Dirt poor. Dirt floor.

That'll be them now if I'm not mistaken. That's a taxi pulling up outside. They're here. I've got to get to the phone.

Ditditdit dotdotdot ditditdit dotdotdot. You are coming into danger! Danger! Danger! Danger! Oh! ditditdit dotdotdot ditditdit!

Four Dresden china figurines in crinolines—one red, one white, one blue and one pink—roll around on the table. They roll to the four corners of the table, the four points of the compass, and come to rest against a white picket fence—of teeth.

That's the taxi door slamming shut. They'll be here any minute. I've got to get to the phone.

Ditditdit dotdotdot ditditdit!

That's the squeak of the front gate being opened. I've got to get to the phone. That's the squawk of the front gate being closed. She must have changed, she always left it swinging open, just to annoy. I've got to get to the phone.

The figurines are turned over. They are hollow inside. The figurines try, frantically, to make themselves decent but their ineffectual windsock arms won't work to hide their shame.

You can see right up our big-hooped skirts. I just want the earth to open up so I can fall in. I can't hide my shame.

That's them walking on my new white, Granetic crushed granite path. I've got to get to the phone.

And there, inside each of the skirts, is a mad little black homunculus creature running like crazy, turning each skirt into a pet exercise wheel. As the skirts spin around and around they become monstrous puppets, helplessly being blown clock-wise, then anticlockwise like spinifex. Their gigantic windsock arms, made from plastic garbage bags, flap around; aimless, sinister.

Run, run, as fast as you can. You can't catch me, I'm the Gingerbread Man.

Every night when Daddy comes home, the monkey's on the table. Get a stick and give her a poke. Pop goes the weasel.

I can hear their voices climbing up the front steps. I've got to get to the phone.

Dittydittyditty dottydottydotty dittydittyditty dottydottydotty!

The round table has become a circular patch of cleared earth. The crystal basket full of gold plastic wheat stalks has become a brass and stone sculpture like the brass memorials you sometimes find on tourist trails to mark important historical spots—part Foundation Stone, part memorial sundial, part compass, part barbecue.

All brass. All brass. All brass.

An ancient campfire is etched into the brass. There are arrows of a compass also etched into the edges of the brass plaque. These four arrows point to the four crinolined figurines at the edge of the clearing.

The skirts stop rolling around and come to a stop with the hollow bottoms of their skirts facing towards the centre of the clearing. They have become humpies. The homunculus creatures stop their frantic running and start crying out, 'Black. Deaths. In. Custard-y. Black. Deaths. In. Custard-y.'

Each skirt is hemmed with a circle of white picket-fence teeth. The homunculus creatures lift their t-shirt tops and point to their Black-skin chests, making the Black pride sign Nicky Winmar made on the football field.

The bare brown dirt has now become multicoloured clays. The crinolined figurines have become four corrugated-iron and bark humpies.

All the colours of the land. All the colours of the rainbow. At the four corners of the compass.

The brass memorial has now become the stone-cold ashes of an Aboriginal campfire. Four huge yellow bulldozers move out from these ashes towards each of the crinoline/humpies—to the four points of the compass. The bulldozers just knock into the crinoline/humpies, just knock them over to reveal large rectangular holes, like mass graves, where each crinoline/humpy has stood. Beaming up out of each grave-hole is a powerful, rich, bright golden light. And then a voice, that emanating from the deep earth booms out from four old-fashioned megaphones like open black mouths, on telegraph poles above each open grave.

'This is the Voice of Radio Moses on Permanent Wave. I give unto you, free and gratis, the Last-Straw Law of the Land. All the evidence is in; now there's no excuse. You know. The sin(ce) of the past. You must eat the earth of the place you've planted yourself. Paydirt. You must carry your kill home to Cook and you must carry it unto(ld) generations. Still born. Still born. Still born. You are peopled improperly. Still birth. Still birth. Still birth.'

Mum gave me this silver locket for my thirteenth birthday. She'd put one of my baby curls inside.

Frizzy black hair spills out of the locket. It spills out all over Dellmay's hands, spills all over the table, the carpet, the room. Look closely, the hair is a mad little cowhair lure scribbling itself everywhere in crazy copperplate.

There's no way in the world—Mum always had the most beautiful copperplate hand.

You are coming into danger. Danger! Danger! Danger!

'… please darling, I'd give anything in the world if you'd go into your little room and put this beautiful frock on and come out and wait on the couch with Daddy and I ... everyone back where they belong ... everything back in its proper place ... you see it's never too late ... darling, you mightn't understand why we've done what we've done, but—'

Leave me out of this, woman.

'... your father's been no help at all, as usual ... but once you're back in your own little room again, and once Warren is back where he belongs, safe and happy with others like himself, you'll see how right I was ... I know you better than you know yourself darling ... Daddy and I love you so very much and all we've ever wanted to do is protect you from yourself ... now, will you do just one thing for Mummy and Daddy? ... if you only knew how much we'd love you to go in and put on that lovely frock I made you ... is that too much to ask? ... it would make us so very happy.'

Leave me out of this, woman.

'... and then come and sit in the lounge room with Daddy and I like you used to ... you don't know what it means to me to have Daddy and you both back where you belong ... surely you see now that a mother—'

S-s-smother.

'... only has her daughter's best interests at heart ... do you still have your lovely naturally wavy hair? ... your migraines? ... your stoop? ... have you kept up your sewing? ... your piano? ... do you still have that capillary problem with your right eye? ... that displaced fontanelle?'

All that can be heard in the darkness is the sound of a truck labouring along a lonely dirt road and the sound of water pouring down.

PAYDIRT—*immutable rubric. Bloodweeping earth—held in the hand. Landgrab—in perpetuity. Consecrate this ground,* *this earth, this air, this us. To touch is to consecrate. Do not do it lightly. Hammer it home. Tamp it down. Get stuck in. We must eat the earth of the place we've planted ourselves. The place you'll bury us. It always all comes down to the land in the end and the earth is aboriginal.* PAYDIRT. PAYDIRT. PAYDIRT.

The front doorbell plays a ridiculous medley of 'Rule Britannia' and 'Waltzing Matilda'.

That'll be them now.

Everyone brings us happiness.

Some as they arrive.

Some as they leave.

I've put the fish fingers out to defrost.

The gloves are off.

Quick Mum! Get the gun! There are Blacks about! I can smell em.

The niggers are in the woodpile! There's a boongaroo loose in the top paddock!

Nigger! Nigger! Pull the trigger.

HAPPY-GO-LUCKY
(English language title)

AU KOSKIRIA MIR
(Meriam Mer—Eastern Islands language title)

WANGAI KEDTHA KAZ
(Kala Lagaw Ya—Western Islands language title)

'Thank you nurse. Nothing stronger than black tea in here I suppose? Oh well! It'll still buck me up.'

They'll be here soon. Better spruce myself up a bit. Bit a lippy. I don't want to look too much of an old reef wreck. I thought I'd left all this behind long ago on Thursday Island. My Bub, no she calls him his proper name, Warren, Warren will be walking in that door any time now. My poor baby. I can't believe it, I thought I'd never see him again but all that shame and heartbreak will be walking in with him too. He thinks his father will be here. I couldn't tell him about Albert on the phone. And he keeps arksing all those questions. I don't know what to tell him. I never thought I'd have to explain all that to anyone, wanted it all to die and be buried in the grave with me. And that Kate, that white woman, she'll smile that Kole smile at me, Warren's Black mother, but I'll bet she'll be thinking, 'Look at that rubbish. Couldn't even look after her own kid. Look at that golliwog.'

'Frangipani Land every day a joy for living
and sweet voices fill the air
that surrounds this tiny island
it is T. I. and that is why
I love my Frangipani Land'

Frangipani Land? Bullshit Land more likely. Just took off into the blue in that little white plane and I've only ever been back the once. Bullshit Land alright. Tried never to think about any of it again. It wasn't such a bad place before the war. Everyone knew their place till they let the Islanders onto Thursday Island and all the grog and that started. That's when it all started going downhill.

La cook-a-racha, la cook-a-racha.

Gee Bub, I mean, Warren, remembered me telling him everyone called me La cook-a-racha from that first phone call. Seeing him again it's bringing it all back. I haven't been called that in years. It was the only good thing I could think to tell him when he was arksing me all those questions. And it's true I was the best cook on the Island and everyone used to sing out to me like that, 'Yawal La Cook-a-racha!' He's asking about his father, the Island—he thinks I still live there and am going to take him back with me. Gee he sounds like Albert though. He's Albert's son alright. Stupid bugger never believed it. The cause of everything, that.

La cook-a-racha, la cook-a-racha.

But this Kate? Don't know what to make of her. Is she from the Gubberment? I thought she said she was his foster mother? But if she is I can't make any sense of what Warren was saying on that TV program. I was that shocked just suddenly looking up from the Pokies and seeing my Bub on TV. I knew him straight away. I was winning, too, that day—on Lucky Number 13, as usual. It upset me so much when he said how his foster mother stole him from his tribe and locked him in a chicken coop in the backyard and fed him slop-slop like a dog and stopped him coming back to us and won't let him come home now. She didn't sound that bad on the phone. I wonder if this Kate was the one that social worker said wanted to adopt him outright all those years ago. That rotten white bitch of a social worker said he was a vegetable and I should thank God some do-gooder was stupid enough to want him. Oh well, I'll be finding out soon enough.

Thirteenth child of a diabetic mother. That's what was on the file. Lucky Number 13 I called him, my Miracle Bub. Had him after my tubes were tied. Some doctors. Yeah! And some mother.

I'd lost so many by the time you came along, Bubs. Sometimes before I even showed, sometimes they just come along and cry a bit, hang on a while and then just die. But they were still born. Yes, still borne. Our kids just died, our babies just died in those days. No one really knew why or told us why—the water, the mosquitoes, something in our blood, God's will. I guess we were just Black and nobody cared.

La cook-a-racha, la cook-a-racha.

And when I asked him if he'd ever tasted earth-oven dugong he said, 'Not as yet Mum.' He talks real well, you wouldn't think there was a thing wrong with him. I said we'd cook him up a real kupmarie feast at Christmas when he comes up to Cairns. And we'll dance. Get a pig and the boys can go out and catch turtle and dugong and fish. I'll make up turtle blood sausage, sweet potato and pumpkin sop-sop, cook it up in coconut juice and wrap it up in banana leaves. Oh! and mud clam blatchan, damper, ooh and molasses damper, sabee sabee kumala, numus kennilau, dinagwan, num lights—real kai-kai. I've been cooking steak and chips and roast and chips for so long now.

'I'll cook up some real kai-kai for you, hey Bub. I mean, Warren.'

La cook-a-racha, la cook-a-racha.

La cook-a-racha, la cook-a-racha.

That smoke must be getting in my eyes, the first kupmarie he goes to will probably be my tombstone opening feast. Oh well!

'... no love, it wasn't eating no 'wonky berry' hurt your poor head ... you pronounce it 'wongai fruit', Bub ... and eating it's supposed to make you want to go back to the Islands, that's the legend anyway ... how can I ever tell you what really happened? ... the doctors reckoned you had meningitis, that's what's on the file and that's what your Mum would think too, and I want to leave it like that.'

What good would it do raking up the rotten old past? I blamed Albert and everyone else on the Island blamed him. Only his drunken friends talk to him after what he did, nobody else. Nobody talk to me any more either. It was awful. And I blame myself too, it's at least half my fault, if I hadn't been sitting there at the Federal flirting with those whitefellas that night—I still don't know the real reason for Bubs going back to babyhood but I just wish Albert knew that the boy had come good. Poor old Albert went to his grave with all the guilt and the sadness. It's what killed him really. He was a real old Islander, I can tell Bub that. No, call him Warren.

'... Albert came from Mabuiag, Warren ... a real Mabuiag man ... initiated, everything ... when any of you kids were naughty I'd say, 'It's the Mabuiag headhunter coming up in you.' ... and he'd get that wild ... but it was true ... but smart! ... when I first knew him ... when we were first married ... he had such a beautiful copperplate hand and he could spell anything.'

I can tell Warren about that. But we weren't allowed to go beyond Grade Three in those days. My Albert tried to do so many things but was always stymied in the end. If he'd been a white man he could have done almost anything, so many ideas in that Kuiam head of his. 'Hey! Kuiam!' I'd say to him, and rub his tight curly head. 'Kuiam's head's a good head, a head teeming with ideas, a clever head.' And he'd say, 'Not like ours, which are bad, stupid, useless heads.' 'Kapi kuik, wakain tamamal kuik, kutinaaa kuik, wati kuikul, boma kuikul, kutingi kuikul.' That was from a poem he wrote too. That's how clever he was then. And later on he'd recite it but he'd be hitting his head with his fists or against the wall. Last time I tried to patch things up by calling him Kuiam he was crying and saying, 'No Plorence, nor caller me Kuiam I gard noo good ed. Plorence, nor caller me Kuiam, nor more. Mine is a bad, stupid, useless head.' And he started banging his head on the wall. We always got too much drink aboard but after what he did to Bubs we got really stuck in. Albert neber itter picnini blo m before, m be drink too muss, en m e prupper jelous me when I talk too long, talk where dem Kole in the Federal Hotel.

'… if your father was alive now Warren, he'd say he was sorry for what he did, I know he would … he'd never hurt any of you kids before and that was the first and last time … I couldn't stand him near me after that … there are some things a woman just can't forgive even if she wants to … no Bub it wasn't eating no 'wonky berry' … what can I tell you when you arks all those questions?'

That night, after we carry Albert home from the Federal and he comes to, he get proper wild. He was on top step and e graber Bub and he chuckaway Bub down the step. Down then hitter head on groun, yelling that he wasn't his kid. I never calla police, never calla doctor. I wanna calla doctor but no them policeman come take Albert. I don't want him to go jail. He never do this thing before. I pickem up Bub, take em inside, make em lay down. Bub proper still, no move, no nothing. Try pickimup Bub, no noise, no sound come from Bub. I think oh he sleep so I put him back in bed. Bub lie down couple a days, I think I betta see doctor and doctor say something very wrong with him, baby very sick, he just lie there with a fever and they think he's going to die.

After a couple of months, when he got a bit better, I'd go down to the hospital. He just screamed and cried and banged his little head and hit out and no one could get near him so they asked me to come down to feed him. As I'd walk up to the room he was in I'd hear the terrible moaning and I'd make the family whistle and the moaning would stop and he'd cock his head to one side and look up with that blank, empty face and he'd sort of half crawl, half walk over to me and he'd take my hand and smell it. I happy he still know me but I think my poor baby, I proper sorry for him, proper sorry. Not my Bub any more. I couldn't stand it after a few days and I'd send one of the kids. That's when I really got stuck into the drink. Not for the fun of it any more. No matter how much I drank it was never fun for me any more after that. My poor baby. I can never tell you all that Bub, never, just say meningitis like file say. You love your father and I know you'd hate him if you knew what he did. Just kept thinking all those years it would get better and one day you just know it never will, no matter how happy you try to make yourself. You know something's gone too far and then once you see it somehow it just keeps going. You think it can't get worse and then it does and it just goes on and on. But Warren coming back like this, that might put a stop to it. It doesn't hurt so much to remember now, knowing he's OK.

I don't think Albert want to brain-damage Bub but he did and I hate him for that, I really hate him, and I could never forgive him for that. I never spoke to him again. I took off down south. Got a job cooking. Made another life. Islanders call me a Mainland Torres Strait Islander now, full of white ways, Aborigines call me 'mud', Kole calls me 'abo' or 'boong' or they're too nice to me, just keep smiling at me. Really haunts me, that whitefella smile. I get proper wild inside.

'… the family really broke up after what happened to you Bub … we all went our separate ways after you were taken south … the boys went on the merchant navy … your Dad went south to Mackay cane-cutting, then on the wolfram mine … anything he could get … then laying the line to Port Hedland … until he got real bad … got stuck into the metho … didn't even have a drink price by then … and that was the finish of him … got the Horrors, everything … his drinkin days were over … we didn't have the money to send him back home … and so he's buried a long way from home … we gave him the tombstone opening over there at Port Hedland cemetery … got a real home there and at peace now, I hope.'

I can tell Warren that. Show him the photos of us all at that tombstone opening. Oh but I might scare him talking about a 'tombstone opening', might think we open that grave up or something pagan like that.

'… that tombstone opening ceremony is very important to us Warren … all the family chips in and buys the best tombstone we can … with a photo of the person and verses about them on it … and then we dress that tombstone with material and flowers and raffia and put presents around it from the family for everyone who comes … it's beautiful … we sing hymns and songs and say goodbye for the last time to that person we loved and even though we're sad, we're happy too because that person has a home now, forever … and then we have a big kupmarie feast.'

I'm sorry about it all Albert, that you went to your grave not knowing Bub was OK or what had happened to him. I'm sorry I was a torment to you love and just thought of having a good time.

La cook-a-racha, la cook-a-racha.

The teacher, Sir, he liked me to call him 'Sir', Sir used to call me his 'silly little cricket' from the poem he liked to recite to us about this ant and this cricket, 'Not a crumb to be found on the snow-covered ground', and he laughed when I said, 'But there's no snow-covered ground here Sir.' But he still made me stay in after school all by myself and write, 'If you live without work, you will die without food' twenty times on the blackboard while he watched, and that—

still born still born still born
still birth still birth still birth
that was my first

La cook-a-racha, la cook-a-racha.

I'll cook him up some belly pwaka. Crush up some soya beans and garlic in soya sauce and vinegar and rub it into the meat then fry the slices in hot oil for about fifteen minutes till they're brown, oh yeah! With fried potato and shallots. He'll love that one.

Albert used to love the sea. I can tell Bub about that. Said he loved under the sea, not so much on top. That once you knew under, well—he'd say, 'When you're down that deep, right on the floor it's brighter than daylight. As you go down you go into the dark, then into the light, then into the dark again.' He was always under the sea diving for crays or for pearls. Dived all his life. He was so good the army paid him to dive for gold-lip, silver-lip, black-lip and cowrie during the war. They used that like real money, to pay the New Guinea blokes. 'Fuzzy wuzzy angels', they called them, who'd only work for shell, real old Blackfellas. Saw it on TV the other night. Some of them still can't understand why pictures on bits of paper are more valuable than the things themselves. And when you think about it they've got a point. Still pay for things in shell and pigs' tusks. Good for them!

> 'I'll bring you some turtle eggs
> they're very good
> I'll bring you some crocodile eggs
> they're very good
> I'll bring you some pigeon eggs
> they're best of all'

That's the first thing he ever said to me, another poem of his. Whispered it really. Snuck up behind me and whispered it in that soft, sexy voice of his. Same voice as Warren's. Gee! I haven't forgotten anything. All that rubbish I went with hoping I'd feel that Kuiam feeling again like I felt with Albert, but no, I never did. I was sitting on the beach there, down from the Federal, looking over the Strait, trying to get a bit of evening breeze off the water. The police found us that night. Took me home and I got a real flogging from Mum. Albert got locked up and they gave him one of those old-time haircuts, half his hair off. They did that to us then if they found boys and girls even talking to each other. I got put in jail for kissin a boy after a dance when they took us down to Cherbourg during the war. And that's all we did, kiss, one little peck. But someone told and

I'm in jail for two days. My first kiss, not even sweet sixteen. But nobody could kiss like Albert. He was that handsome and strong—strong in his mind, real mind power that man had, and strong in his body too. He'd been watching me on the sly for ages and I played hard to get. Then he got the courage up to get my best friend, Sarita, to tell me to meet him. Passed her a note for me, passed her a couple. Anyway, Albert wouldn't see me for ages for shame having his hair like that. We eventually got together. I really loved Albert and he loved me back but we were never so free and easy with each other again after that night.

'... I'd like to be able to tell you all this love, but I can't, it's just sad old stuff best left unsaid ... let sleeping dogs lie as they say ... things were so hard for us on the Islands then but I'll take it all to the grave with me ... but poor old Albert, he had to go down, cap in hand, and beg Mr Brisbane, he was the Protector the Queensland Government had sent up to look after us, had to beg that old Brisbane for us to get married because of the Act, the Dog Act we called it ... everyone reckoned I married down to marry Albert ... see Albert was under the Dog Act because he was full Islander but I wasn't ... we didn't even really question it at the time, it was just the way it was ... even though my mother was an Islander my father was another islander, an Irishman from the Emerald Isle ... I can tell you about that, Bub ... but he left before I was born ... 'La Captain Cook-a-racha, la Captain Cook-a-racha', that's what they'd call out if they wanted to have a go at me about having a white father but I didn't care, just laughed and ignored them.

I got adopted, Islander style, by Malays, so became, officially, on paper anyway, a Malay too ... Islanders called me outcast, Malays called me bingai, dirty Islander, but I didn't care, Mum and Dad were beautiful people and I always kept happy-go-lucky … yes, I can tell you about Mum and Dad, Bub.

'… because I was officially a Malay I had lots of privileges the real Islanders didn't have … one thing, I could drink in the pubs and that … it was really because of that that that bad thing happened with you, Warren love … Albert fought for his country, your father fought for his country, Bub … and yet he couldn't even come in and have a drink decent with his wife, with the mother of his kids … him, looking in through the window at me laughing and flirting and me having to sneak grog out to him out there … and I was that wild in those days and wanted a good time, to have a bit of fun after working in that hot kitchen all day and there were only the pubs really to enjoy yourself … same as now, pubs and churches only places to get together … still not that different up there … cops still chasing Islanders across the Sports Field there by the school … caught one of us too just before I went up last time … some young fella … I don't like to even think his name … on his nineteenth birthday …. same birthday as Prince William … but our young boy wasn't photographed playing polo with his father … no … he was chased across the Sports Field and run down by the cop car … he was photographed lying dead on the Sports Field … right near the fence.'

No, can't tell Bub all this sad old stuff. It'll just frighten him. We always called it the Sports Field, not because we played polo or cricket on it, oh no, not on your life. We called it that because that has always been the sport of the cops, to chase us across that field. Don't know how many times they chased me across that field, never caught me though, I always got to that fence, over it and away. That lad must have slipped or something.

He nearly made it. If he'd gotten to that fence he'd have been into the bush and away. Don't know what happened about that in the end. There was some kind of Inquest into it. Last I heard all the cops were transferred off the Island, no charges laid, etcetera etcetera. Those Islanders probably think that was some kind of victory. Ah well! Anyway, nobody will talk about it any more. Let sleeping dogs lie. That's the mentality.

Oh Albert! I was a torment to you, I see that now, especially when I was full of the drink. How can I explain all that to the boy? How bad it was for us up there then. How things just got out of hand. You can't imagine things can get worse, then they do.

La cook-a-racha, la cook-a-racha.

I'll cook him up some cassava doughboys in coconut milk and sugar. He'll really love that.

Albert would have to go down, cap in hand, to ask Mr Brisbane for his pay. Lousy little bit he got too. Work hard for bloody months and then, under the Dog Act, can't even get the miserable little bit. Real Kole he was, that Chief Protector, liked to be carried from his boat to the beach so his pants don't get wet. And some of the Islanders, monkey-men, yes-boss men, they were proud to carry him too. 'He knows me,' they say proudly. Still people like that now who are proud to be seen with whitefellas, have whitefella friends and I'm a bit like that myself with my whitefella boyfriends. Put up with a lot, more than I ever should have, felt so proud to have a white man want me. Funny isn't it, white women love a Blackfella, 'Once you try Black you never go back', I've heard them say and us Black women love the white boys.

There were always boys after me, with my red hair and my blue-green Irish eyes. I liked playing the field. Dancing and drinking and flirting. Called myself Slap-Happy-Go-Lucky, in the end, I got slapped that much by those women for playing up with their men. I liked those Bank boys too. Stupid really but there you are. I liked those white boys and they liked me back. That one, in the end, would have married me too but the Bank found out about us and next day he'd just gone. Been transferred or promoted or something. So I suppose it was lucky I lost that baby too.

Still bank with the Commonwealth. I always think I'll run into him one day just going into the Bank. The Bank that says 'Yes'. I liked that ad, always gave me a laugh.

That Kate wants to know who rang her up last week. Should I tell her how Aunty Iris found them? Hacked into the data bank in the computer at the Department where she works and found his number and rang. Iris knew I wanted to see Warren before I went. I'm real sick this time, real sick. Doctors don't hold out much hope. No, I can't tell her that, get Iris into trouble if anyone finds out. She might lose her job. No, just say the yam-vine. Might tell her later on. Kate took down the number of the hospital and rang the next day. Gee I was that shocked and surprised. We didn't know what to say to each other and then she put Warren on and oh my God, there was no trouble with him. He says, first thing, clear as anything, you wouldn't think there was a thing wrong with him, he says, 'Hello there Mum! Long time no see in a bunch of Sundays.' Well, laugh—I laughed till I cried. And he did too. Real Islander that boy. Got a real Islander sense of humour. They said they were taking him away to get good medical treatment and good education. They never said it would be for good.

'... you want to know your father's name, love ... as far as I know Albert was just Albert ... that's all I ever called him but I'm sure he had another Islander name ... all I know is that Albert liked being called Albert ... he was embarrassed with his Islander name ... I heard people from Mabuiag calling him by that name sometimes but I can't speak that Kala Lagaw Ya language ... only know a little bit from the little song he taught you ... he was that proud of you ... called you 'young Kuiam' ... said you were the smartest of all the kids learning all those words like that.'

> 'awaial gar naki, awaial gar naki
> bal paganu padal awaial e.
> ply por nothing e, ply por nothing e.
> big mouth, small eyes, small kubalab
> dukaw ngaral nga'

> La cook-a-racha, la cook-a-racha.

I can cook him up some pumpkin pakalolo. Grate the pakalolo and put it in some water then squeeze it through a cloth until all the juice is out. And then just leave that juice till the pakalolo starch settles on the bottom then pour off that water and mix up the pakalolo starch with the pakalolo mash and some flour and salt and sugar and some cooked pumpkin. And lemon rind. It's easy to forget that lemon rind. And bake it in the oven for about three hours and then you take it out and pour coconut milk over it while you cut into it with a really sharp knife. You've got to do it while it's real hot though so the coconut oil will be soaking through it while the milk cooks. And then you serve it beside fish or meat or whatever. I'll make him some pumpkin pakalolo. He'll love that one.

'You are like my beautiful home, Mabuiag.' I've still got that letter where Albert wrote that to me. I've still got it somewhere. 'She is also a fair and beautiful woman with greenery jewellery of tropical life, sitting like we do at sunset, facing the right way, facing the southeastern horizon and feeling the southeast wind on our faces. And the rising and falling of the tide makes her sink to her waist. Your hair is like the coconut palms.' I remember it by heart because I used to scream it at him in the end, throw it all back in his face, when he'd drag me into the yard by that coconut hair that he loved so much. 'The two tips of Cape Panai and Cape Sipi ngurr are the arms of this fair woman embrace.' Gee he was so talented, singing and dancing and he wrote songs, painting, writing, you name it. All the Islanders are like that though. But we weren't even allowed to go past Grade Three in those days or go to the Mainland to that Keo Deudai. Albert never called it Australia or the Mainland, always that Keo Deudai. Reckoned one of his ancestors was an Aborigine who'd married a Mabuiag woman and had that baby Kuiam. Might be why Warren can play that didg so well. I can show Warren the painting. Oh! He probably won't be able to see it, but he might. He tells me he's not totally blind yet. The diabetes hasn't got that far. He was that excited when I told him I'd had toes off, said he was just like me, a real Islander, because he almost had his whole leg off with something he called gang-of-green new-moan-new off-the-bone, I guess he meant gangrene. Said they won't get his toes though because he never takes his Blundies off, even in bed. What's that Kate up to, letting him sleep with his boots on? Gee whiz! Anyway, at least I can recite Albert's poem to him. 'Arms of this fair woman embracing me as if I'm the village snuggling into the Bay of—' No! Shame! I'll keep the rest to myself.

La cook-a-racha, la cook-a-racha.

'cakaros e run untup my hand, kempo era tag e
cakaros e run untup my hand, kara barada
kempo era tag e
I tarai waneea pattea em
emi go undanit, undanit ene tabol e'

'... I met Albert just after the war, Bubs, Warren, no, Bub
... that war got us all thinking in one way or another really
... changed the place ... I met Albert just after they'd brought
us back from down south and Albert and ... that's right, there
was Ted Loban and Joe Ah Mat ... they'd come back in their
uniforms ... money in their pocket ... good as any white man
and they knew it ... those white soldiers were really disgusted
the way we were treated, not getting paid properly and that
... and we were real sick of it too ... Albert used to say, 'Sea,
land and everything is ours. Those Kole they come and go
and take everything out, never bring anything good back. We
fight. We always fought but the government is on their side. Do
everything in that hidden language.' ... anyway Ted and Joe and
I and Jumulla ... that's right, Jumulla Dubbins was one of the
ring leaders ... named that hostel up there after Jumulla ... we
geed ourselves up to have a go at that old picture theatre there
on the corner of, what was it now? ... anyhow, just near where
the Chinese gambling place was and the opium place ... anyway
they had this sign there outside saying **WHITES UPSTAIRS** and we
organised a demonstration I suppose it would be called now ...
long before that Freedom Ride Charlie Perkins organised for
Aborigines ... Islanders doin it for themselves as usual, same
as Koiki Mabo ... and anyway nobody went in for a week or

more and finally the Manager took down the sign ... the whites still went upstairs and we went down but we'd made our point ... nobody much remembers that now ... or even wants to as far as I can tell, 'We're all friends here now,' that's what you hear those monkey-men saying ... and that big white Haradine Hotel ... big white insult I reckon ... that old Haradine was a magistrate and a murderer ... everyone knows he killed plenty of Blackfellas but they sit in the aircon, swim in that stupid little pool and drink ... but not me, I got the willies just seeing that name ... not me I been down south too long and I know too much about freedom now ... they don't want to remember those days, 'There was never any of that racism stuff here,' they say ... but it's true what I'm saying ... but—'

No need to tell the boy that stuff. Take it to the grave with me untold, I suppose. The tennis club was the worst. We'd stand outside and look in at the dances but it was whites only. They wouldn't say that out loud but Joe decided to test it one night. He got all dressed up beautifully and he and Jumulla, so stylish on his arm—she'd send away from the Catalogue for her dresses—tried to go in but they wouldn't let them in. Just stopped them on the steps. Just wouldn't let them in, so what else could it be but racism pure and simple. And those same white boys wouldn't mind meeting us girls in the dark afterwards though, after they'd dropped off their dates. Islanders did this tennis dance once. It was that beautiful and funny. Don't know where they got all the rackets though. I'd love to see that one again.

The ABC interviewed me while I was there, about those old days. I told them all that stuff but when the ABC showed it to the elders that afternoon in the Gateway Hotel over on Horn Island they said to take mine out. Didn't like what I said. Said they didn't want to make trouble. Some of them even walked out. All mates with whitefellas now.

I'll never go back there again though, that's where all the shame is. But it's down here now, with Warren and this white woman, his mother, Kate, Mum. But I can't tell her about all that. That white woman will look at me and that shame will come again. I could tell her about Islander adoption, that I was adopted too and that when a kid is adopted Islander-way the mother never comes and takes that kid or anything, that new mother is the real mother. She's my son's mother so I call her 'Mum'. She probably doesn't know about that.

I'll never go back up there again. Last time I was up on the Island for my aunty's tombstone opening I vowed I'd never go up again. Down here I'm an Islander, up there I'm just a trouble-making Mainlander. One old fellow told me, to my face, to go back where I came from. And it's true I've got a different way of seeing things after all these years down south. I said to him, 'You ought to be ashamed of yourself letting your wife do all the work, carry those heavy bags, walk behind you.' That's one thing, Albert would never let me walk behind him like that, always held my hand in public, walking down the street, never had that attitude to me like I was beneath him somehow because I was a woman. Anyway, that old fellow, you know what he said to me, he said, 'Flo, go back where you came from. That's the way we do things on the Island.' All these women on the outer Islands, carrying firewood and that on their backs, looking after the kids, doing all the work, the gardening and cooking and that, and the men sitting in the shade singing and learning the dances. Like Ellie Gaffney in her book about the women doing all the work and then the men taking over and being chairmen and that of organisations. I go back there now and they call me a

Mainlander. Down here I'm an Islander or a Boong or a Nigger, up there I'm not even an Islander any more I'm a Mainlander with whitefella ways, a coconut, black on the outside, white on the inside.

Oh! I don't want to go back there any more. I'm scared of that puri-puri. They still do that, and I tell you it works. I went to the feast and I saw all those women and one of them sent one small girl over with a drink. She said, 'Here aunty.' I asked her, 'Who this from?' She pointed at a woman who hadn't liked me since she reckoned I was after her man thirty years or more ago. That's what they're like, thirty years and still carrying that grudge. Nothing better to do up there I suppose. And I thought, 'Ooh!' and I didn't drink any of it, just pretended to, and later I pretended I dropped it on the floor and spilt it. I wasn't game to drink anything. By the end of the night I was that thirsty I got sick from dehydration, so I suppose that puri-puri works.

I was just looking over at this couple one day, thought I knew them, and the woman came over and slapped my face. True! She said, 'You after my man? You having an affair with my man or something?' I said, 'I don't even find him interesting. I'm not attracted.' And she slaps me again. That's the Islands for you, have to be real careful even seen talking to a man. Those women come and bash you, make puri-puri and can even kill you.

People think the race thing's gotten better down here but it hasn't really. One day I was going to work and the Inspector took my ticket, clicked it and then threw it onto the floor. I've never heard an Asian girl swear but this young Chinese woman next to me said, 'Don't pick the bloody thing up. What a bitch to do that.' And I said, 'I have to. I have to. I have to get to work.' I should have left it there. I let an Asian girl stand up for me and I didn't myself. That's shame! That's shame!

Or, people are too nice to me down here they just keep smiling at me. I hate that stupid Kole smile they give you when they don't even know you from Adam. They don't even know you and they give you that big, stupid smile. Rather they hit me than that, don't know how to fight that. Like this one woman at work said to me, trying to be nice I suppose, that I must have a wonderful sense of rhythm and be in touch with my spirituality. She asked me a few times to come to one of her Saturday afternoon 'at-homes' she called them. Said she wanted her kids to experience every culture before they went to university, liked to have all sorts, and she'd never had an Islander. Asked me if I could wear my hoola skirt. I've never worn a hoola skirt in my life.

And I forgot about all those cockroaches and mosquitoes up there. They're that big! And there was even a crocodile alert at the beach one day. No fear, I'm used to the south now. It's all changed so much. Hear kids swearing and that in front of the old people. I was so shocked, at the tombstone feast, they brought a lot of those old people to the feast. Drove them in the minibus from Star of the Sea home but, when the feast came out, nobody served those old people. Everyone just rushed onto that food just like all those big greedy blowflies the young girls were trying to swish off with those bunches of leaves. Plates high with it and only a couple of us looked after those old people. No, I'll never go back there, not after seeing all I saw last time. Saw it all in a different light, just used to take it all as normal before. Things were bad back when I was young but not that bad, that's not the way we were taught. And those same people with their plates high and stuffing their own mouths, next thing there's all this bullshit about Islanders being caring and sharing and looking after the family and that. And the real Islanders, like Albert, sitting around the edge taking the leftovers after the whitefellas and Malays take their share. I was sitting with Sarita having a cup of coffee in one of the grotty little cafes looking onto the main street and she kept saying how different it was now, that 'they' were everywhere, that 'they' had houses built for them right on T. I. now and things like that. I was only half listening and then I realised when she said 'they' she meant Islanders. If I'd stayed there I'd probably have been just like that too. No Warren love, don't reckon I'll be taking you back there.

And then again nothing much has changed at all, like the thirties up there. Lot of those women are scared and kept down by those men and get bashed and are scared shitless, like I used to be of Kevin. I went with him after I left the Island. He was a white man, a lot younger. I thought he was lovely—blond hair—and he was nice to me at first but then he got on the drink too. Well that's where we met so I suppose I should have known. Met down at the Club and I was putting the coins in. When I finally did leave him I had to sneak away with the kid while he was at work. He'd brought a mate home to sleep it off the night before and at breakfast I did something wrong—served the small girl first before him because she was whingeing—and he just punched me in the stomach and I went down and he kicked me. Like a wild thing. And his mate whispered to me as he was leaving, 'Get out Flo. Just take the kid and go before he kills you both.' And I did. But he found me and used to wait outside with a rifle. We'd sit in the dark and I'd hear him going around the house and tapping on the windows and that. My little girl told me later he'd been messing with her too when I was out at work and that. She was terrified of him. Thought of Sir again when she told me all that. He'd go to jail now for what he did to me and so should Kevin.

There are some things a woman can't forgive a man, even if she wants to. Once he takes your pride away—well, that went a long time ago and I made it again as best I could out of bits and pieces of rubbish like love and sex and work and things. And all the time a woman has to respect a man's pride and not shame him but they never think a woman might have the same pride, exactly the same pride and shame and hurt. No, no man I've ever met anyway, Black or white, wants that much responsibility, to have to consider that.

Still birth. Still birth. Still birth.
Still born. Still born. Still born.

La cook-a-racha, la cook-a-racha.

I'll cook him up some hot kumala and wadali luer. I'll bet he's never tasted that one.

And when I left the Island last time in that little white plane—just flew off into the blue, again, in that little white plane—and we landed at Bamaga, brought it home to me. Up there I was someone, Aunty this, Sis that. People knew me. Soon as I get on the plane I remember I'm nothing but a boong to those white people. The airhostess, Tiffany I think she was called or Jasmine, some stupid Kole name like that, anyway three old Islander women get on from Bamaga. They had their bags full of damper in banana leaves, flower arrangements, that sort of thing. Been to a tombstone feast. And this Tiffany says, 'First on the left', and they just stand there. Don't know their left from their right. True! And she sort of just pushes them in the right direction with that look on her face. Just pushes those old ladies. No respect. No shame. And we're all trying not to look at them trying not to look at all of us trying not to look at them. The woman next to me whispered, 'Wishes she was on some international flight serving men in Armani suits smelling of Aramis. In first class instead of messing around with a bunch of smelly Blackfellas.' And we had a good laugh.

They showed that *Cracks in the Masks* film in the hall when I was up there. I can tell Warren about that. That Ephraim Bani who made it is related to him. He's bringing all the masks and stuff back to the Torres Strait. Some of those Christian people are scared about that pagan stuff coming back to the Islands. 'We're not like that no more. We're civilised now.' Don't like it. Want all those masks and artefacts and things to stay in that styrofoam snow in the basements of those museums in Cambridge and Germany and wherever. They reckon it's not Christian. They reckon that coconut tree that got hit by lightning and then grew in a cross was a big sign from Christ to the Islands. They reckon we're special. I try to be a good Christian woman but it makes me sad though to think of those old Islander spirits all alone over there in those cold, dark cellars staring up with their pearl-shell eyes at the lids of their coffins. 'Under the snow-covered ground, not a flower can they see, not a leaf or a tree.' Never feeling the south-east breeze off the Strait or hearing the dancing and singing. I think of Albert. And I feel like that sometimes myself, especially at night, lying here in this sparkling white hospital bed, like an old, old Islander a long, long way from home and all alone.

'old T. I. my beautiful home
it's the place where I was born
where the moon and stars that shine
make me longing for home
oh T. I. my beautiful home

take me across the sea
over the deep blue sea
darling won't you take me
back to my own T. I.
the sun is sinking farewell.'

La cook-a-racha, la cook-a-racha.

What have they been telling him? He kept saying Kate stole him? They took him because he was so sick and looked really, really bad. If we'd had physiotherapists, speech therapists, special education teachers—the hospital's even got a helicopter now, they tell me, to ferry people back and forth from the Islands. If we'd had help. If I'd only known what to do with him. They never said he'd be gone forever but none of us knew what to do with him looking terrible like that. Whenever I've dreamt about him he's always been like one of those little coconut fibre and cowhair snares I used to make when we lived in Bundaberg. They needed men to work on the sugarcane fields during the war so they sent us there from Cherbourg and Dad cut cane there. I used to make these funny little black fibre dolls. Uncle Tommy used to call them 'Homunculuses'. I'd collect the cow hair caught on the fences from cow tails to make them. I'd set them up in the big old mango tree in the backyard and catch red and green parrots that Mum would make into a stew. White people shamed us about that but it was good stew, cooked with ginger and bird's eye chilli and a bit of vinegar and sugar and prawn paste blatchan. Real Asian spicy like we like it.

La cook-a-racha, la cook-a-racha.

You know, what I'd love to cook him up is my pearl-meat sambal. Haven't tasted that for over thirty years. Those Japanese love it but it costs a fortune now. Can't get the meat since the pearling industry closed down up there. We always had dried pearl meat at home. Those pearl luggers would come in with all that dried pearl meat hanging and drying from the rigging, and our mouths would water. The men would have carefully collected it and hung it up to dry over all those months, knowing we'd be glad of it when they came back. Pearl-meat sambal, I'd nearly forgotten about that. It was Dad's favourite. That would be something special.

What have they been telling him? Bubs never knew either of his grandfathers. Why did he say in that TV program his grandfather taught him the didgeridoo?

'... that's one thing I can tell you Bubs ... I can tell you about your grandfather ... Dad was on the pearlers, love ... one of the best.'

'remember little boys and girls
the oyster manufactures pearls
which shows what grit can do'

I always remember that. Sir got us girls to embroid that on our sewing samplers. That's nearly all I did at school, except learn my letters. *A* like an apple on a twig, *a* says *ah*. *B* like a bat and ball, *b* says *ba*. *C* like a cake with a bite taken out, *c* says *ca*. *D* drags a drum, *d* says *da*. Or like the kids in Bundaberg used to call after us—*a* for abo, *b* for boong, *c* for coon, *d* for darkie. We cut twelve ton of cane a day on that farm in Bundaberg and I remember the owner came over to us one day. Mum was having a rest. And I can still see him saying to Dad, 'Why don't you make your nigger woman help you?' That's the way they spoke to us.

La cook-a-racha, la cook-a-racha, la cook-a-racha.

Dad would come back from those pearling grounds exhausted from those Darnley Deeps. The divers' graveyard they called them. They had to go further and further out, into more and more danger, as the pearl beds got depleted. 'The bends', the most feared words in those days. We whispered it. I'll tell Warren about his grandfather. He was a very famous diver. I can tell him about that. I used to make up songs for him when I was little and he loved me singing them to him. Reckoned I was the smartest of all the grandkids.

schooner, brig, barque, lugger, cutter, ketch
schooner, brig, barque, lugger, cutter, ketch
out-rigger, out-rigger, out-rigger

And I even made up a little diving dance to go with one of the songs. It used to make him laugh and laugh. Dear old fellow he was.

One shake—hit rock bottom. Did that plenty of times. Nobody down here ever understands when I say, 'one shake'. One pull—want to come up. Two pulls—want more air. Three pulls—slacken pipe. Four pulls—buoy. Five pulls—down jib. Six pulls—propeller go ahead. Seven pulls—boat to right. Eight pulls—boat to left. Nine pulls—plenty of shells. Ten pulls—tide changed.

'… your Dad went pearling too for a while, Bubs … and I'd sing and dance for him too … I haven't danced since I left.'

One pull and a shake—bag up. Two pulls and a shake—danger. Three pulls and a shake—haul in pipe. Four pulls and a shake—sand bank. Five pulls and a shake—half jib. Six pulls and a shake—propeller stop. Seven pulls and a shake—boat to left. Eight pulls and a shake—boat too slow. Nine pulls and a shake—about boat. Two pulls, a shake and two pulls—diver go to your right. Three pulls, a shake and three pull—diver go to your left. I asked Albert once what he did down there all that time just hanging in the water, waiting to come up. 'Did a lot of pulling,' he said and laughed and grabbed me. Dirty bugger. God he was a real donkey dick too, makes me hot just remembering it.

The cook ud have to get some hot tea or coffee and some hot food into them and later on down they'd go again. Out there for months. Lots died. And all for those lousy little pearly buttons. Plastics put a stop to all that. And Mr Mikimoto and his cultured pearls.

Dived to forty-five fathoms in those Darnley Deeps. Had to keep your eyes closed to get used to 'The Great Darkness'. You could only stay down for about fifteen minutes. I used to ask Albert what he saw down there in those Darnley Deeps. 'Ah! The Great Darkness,' he'd say. 'Hanging for an hour at five fathoms to stop the bends, glass buoy marking the place, just hangin. And all for the sake of those little pearly buttons.'

It was dangerous work, diving. Thursday Island cemetery's two thousand richer with dead divers. That's what it cost to stay down too long or dive too deep. He used to reckon, 'Those ladies wearing those strings of nice pearls, they should be wearing necklaces of skulls. They the real pagan headhunters.'

'… if he were here now I know he'd sit you down on the woven mat after tea, Bub, and you'd ask him, 'What do you see down there in those Darnley Deeps, Daddy?' … and he'd say, 'Ah! I see The Great Darkness and then The Great Light, my boy. I see warriors rowing out to sailing ships in canoes. We are holding up green coconuts. We are saying, 'We are ready to exchange.' But the white men in the sailing ships are empty-handed. We are holding up green coconuts. We are ready to exchange but there is only fear and hostility in the eyes we meet. Then the storm-wind starts to blow. It keeps blowing and blowing and it carries everything away, away from us, from our islands. And all is taken—all the turtle shell and pearl shell masks, the carvings, the hunting and fishing charms, the turtle and dugong spears, bu shells, dhoeris and dhibal, the headdresses and dancing machines, the coconuts, the turtles and dugong and pearls, turtle-holding fences, stone fish traps, spinning stone tops—and nothing comes back, only sickness and fear and destruction. The sailing ships are full and heavy and fly off with everything.'

'… and you'd say, 'What else do you see hanging down there, just hangin in those Darnley Deeps Daddy?' … 'Ah! In the Great Darkness I am being buried in sand. I am a woman and I am being buried in the sand by my father and my husband. Only my nose pokes out. All the Islander women are being buried in sand. The men are trying to protect me from the bêche-de-mer and trochus-shell hunters, from the pearlers who will take me away for sex and also to work for them. They will carry me away with them and throw me overboard when they are finished with me or get near their own shores.'

'… what else can you see there in those dark Darnley Deep waters Daddy?'

'Ah! In The Great Darkness I see that the bottom of the ocean is covered in a floor of pearl-shell. It is as beautiful as snow and rainbow colours glisten and shine from it but the great storm-wind blows in one direction and rips up this pearl-shell covering. It blows it away in little round buttons, millions and millions of little round pearly buttons like snowflakes and the pearls and all the colours of the rainbow are so beautiful but they all blow away from our islands and we watch and cry and are very sad and we dance our mourning dance.'

'... what else can you see tonight Dad, looking into those Darnley Deeps?'

'Ah! Did you ask me about The Great Darkness again Plorence, my little Plorence? I see string figures being made and unmade, in a sleight-of-hands game, language being made and unmade, a sign-of-hands game. We scratched so many of our untold stories onto the rocks down there for the fishes to read, for the fishes and dugong and shark and turtle to read forever in those Darnley Deeps.

'I see the 'Coming of the Light'.' I'm a little boy and I'm all dressed up in my best clothes and I'm singing hymns about Jesus Saves at the 'Coming of the Light' Festival. But suddenly I am not dressed in my best clean clothes any more I am dressed in my Islander headdress and so forth. The old black and white film has started running backwards and the missionaries scurry backwards from the village, down the road, onto the beach, into their boat and away over the horizon quick smart. I am chasing them with my warrior-spear and club. I am doing a wonderful warrior war dance on the beach as they become a speck on the horizon and are then gone. Then I hear old Reverend Turner shouting, 'Burn the idols. It is the work of the devil!' and all the masks and sacred things that he threw into the fire and burned for his London Missionary Society that time are un-burning. The great pile of artefacts, masks, hunting charms, totems, drums, ornaments and traditional stuff leap out of that bonfire of his, unscathed. The 'Coming of the Light' dance machine folds up like a flower at night and disappears in darkness and all you can hear, all night long, are our songs of triumph and victory being stamped out and chanted.

'As the songs go on I am in a sailing ship flying over the seas in a storm of pearly button snow. I am bringing it all back and I am unwrapping our old turtle-shell and pearl shell masks from styrofoam snow and bubble wrap, sawdust and tissue paper from crates in the cellars of old European museums. They are opening their eyes. They are beginning to hum, beginning to sing, beginning to chant and do their dance. The only snow that is falling now is the sweet-smelling talcum powder the women are sprinkling over their men, sweating as they dance and dance.'

If the masks come back, make the journey back the way they came, if the 'pagan' past comes back—Warren has come back. Shame has come back. But it's not just shame, it's pride. Pride has come back too. Shame and pride. He is now well. The spirit has come back. The spirit is here. Things are returned. Evil is reversed.

'… no one ever died on Dad's boat, Bub … that was one of his great prides … he reckoned he'd learnt all he knew working with those Japanese divers … he had great respect for them … they were the greatest divers, those Japanese men, and they taught Dad everything … he started out just cleaning the pearl shell for them but he got mates with them and they taught him about diving and pearling and navigating and grading the shell … but one night, at the beginning of the war it must have been, way before you were even a glint in your Dad's eye, love, we were woken up with lots of shouting and searchlights and things and there was barbed wire and machine guns around Japtown, Little Yokohama we always called it, and some of those men were our friends ... and Dad's skipper was behind the barbed wire and we saw him clearly in the searchlight and we could only just give a little secret wave and smile ... it was awful ... they were mates ... and that night they were just marching them out ... we heard later they were sent to Hay in New South Wales ... down your way Bubs ... not so different from us later when they sent us to Cherbourg ... and Phyllis Yamashita told me later ... when she came back ... she was married to an Islander you see ... she came back and she'd been there, in Hay, for over four years ... she talked about it a lot but I can't remember much now ... I do remember her telling me the trip down was the worst ... crammed into the anchor box of the ship for nearly two weeks and no fresh water only desalinated that they couldn't stomach without putting Enos in it ... we'd eaten like kings up here ... especially at Christmas ... and it was such a shock for her she said that on Christmas Day they served the poor buggers sour tripe and white sauce ... ugh! it turns my stomach just to say the words ... she put in a claim for all her smashed and looted property, everything ... and she had lovely things that she sent away for from the Catalogue ... everything gone ... broken, looted, ruined ... even most of the house torn down to build huts for the servicemen ... we all had to build up again from nothing ... and then ... after the war the Islanders were allowed onto T. I. and that was the end of Old T. I. really ... for us half-castes and Malays that is ... different place now alright.'

No, Warren doesn't need to know all that sad stuff.

I remembered that awful night again when I saw that *Schindler's List*. How we just watched from our windows, scared for ourselves. And I felt shamed wondering if we were like those German people just watching and not saying or doing anything and our friends and neighbours being just marched away to God knows where, to be killed in some concentration camp maybe, we didn't know. And that was that and they sent those men back to Japan after the war. Some of those men were born on T. I. and imagine just landing in Japan. Couldn't speak the language, nothing. It would have been a foreign country to them. Once, when one of those bombers came over, some of the Islanders reckoned it flew really low and they could see the pilot's face and he waved to them and smiled. Reckoned they recognised him and that he was a diver before the war. They reckoned that's maybe why we weren't really bombed up here. Also reckon maybe there's a Japanese princess or something buried in the cemetery.

They sent us Malays to Cherbourg with the Aborigines. It was so sad to see them all in Cherbourg and not on their land. All bunched together and people who had never been living together. Like how careful it's got to be between Western Islanders and Eastern Islanders and Central Islanders up home and you imagine what if we were all made to live on the same island. Well, that's how the poor Blacks had to learn to live in Cherbourg. But the Islanders weren't taken off our land. We were hemmed in and not allowed to **leave** our islands. And if we did get off we weren't allowed back. Like with Uncle Koiki Mabo. That's one thing he got so mad about. The Queensland Government wouldn't let him back on when his father was so sick and dying so he decided to take it to the law. I bet that Queensland Government wishes they'd let him back on now.

It gives me a laugh thinking about it. He might have just gone fishing on Mer for the rest of his life instead of causing all that trouble for them. Might never have been that Mabo Case if they'd let him go back to Mer when his father was sick. And that's another first for Islanders and the Aborigines taking all the credit. No respect for us.

Sarita was from Badu and she was left there all during the war because she was full Islander. Just left the Islander women and children to their fate, the Gubberment, Mr Protector Sir, did. Took all the able-bodied men who did the fishing and gardening and left the women and children to starve or be bombed. Some Protector hey, yes, and some Gubberment, as the Murries say. The men eventually went on strike about it and eventually the Gubberment sent canned stuff to tide the women and children over. She, Sarita, said they had to hide in caves a lot of the time because they were afraid of the Japanese planes dropping bombs on them or strafing them which they did a couple of times. She told me they weren't even allowed to go fishing or to wear anything colourful. Had to wear these hessian-coloured things as camouflage. God knows how they were supposed to eat. Anyway she said one day she just thought, 'Oh blow it!' She put on her nice red silk frock. I remember that one her father had bought her for the 'Coming of the Light' ceremony the year before she got married. And she said she was out fishing in the lagoon happy-as-larry when she heard those bombers coming. She dived into the water and stayed under with only her nose showing. She laughs at herself now. 'I was that innocent in those days I didn't know they could see me down there like a big red blossoming hibiscus. They must have laughed at the silly native.' Charlie Turner, the only white man to stay behind and try to help the Islanders, told them to wear pegs on a string around their necks at all times. Like some sort of black magic. God knows what use they'd have been. Bite on it if bombs start dropping, I don't know? Silly whitefella telling silly Blackfellas to do silly things I reckon. I always get a good laugh out of it whenever I peg the clothes on the line though. All the women did things for the war. Sarita said they sat around and wove mats and baskets and things like that for the Red Cross to send south and sell. She said they did a lot of praying too and felt like they were doing their bit for the war.

I can tell Warren about his Uncle Koiki. That's one good thing I can tell him and be proud about. Got off the Islands during the war and never really went back. Was working on the Mainland for a long time trying to work with kids. Get our kids educated. Learning about the white ways and that to teach our kids. One day he was at a conference for teachers in Queensland and he was explaining to them what Islander kids needed in the way of teaching and culture and they said, and this is true, he told me in these exact words, they said, 'Why would we spend time with boongs and Black bastards while we have so many of our own to worry about?' When he heard that, of course, being a very touchy issue in his way of thinking, well he got up and did his dance. He said, 'I really thumped the floor and said, 'Who the hell's going to send their kids to be taught by racist people like you bastards?' Real bloody Kole.' And he walked out and, to give credit where credit is due, some of the whitefellas there also walked out with him. And soon after they made a school for Islander kids in Townsville. I'd love to have seen that, him doing his dance, what a performance. He was smashing down the barriers separating the two worlds that Kole had erected. Putting the two worlds together that Kole had kept apart. That's what he did with his life. Warren should be told about him too. He can be real proud there.

The spirit was there. It was the truth speaking.

'... that's the way we were taught to be, Bub ... that's the way the old people taught us ... I'd love you to be sitting down in the dark on the mat after tea, listening to the story those old people are telling ... I've lost those things to tell you ... I haven't got anything to tell you like they told me and I never listened properly, just went my own happy-go-lucky way with the grog and the men and that ... and all **my** sad stories will go to the grave with me ... I'll never burden you with them love.'

La cook-a-racha, la cook-a-racha.

All those years 'protecting' us. Taking our money and telling us where we could and couldn't go and what we could and couldn't do and everything and then the war comes. Bang! Off they go and leave us to the Japanese. Took my Albert and all his brothers and father, and never paid them properly. They built roads, bridges, the dam on Horn, dug wells. Albert learnt how to drive over there and could drive a bulldozer and work jackhammers and compressors and detonators. He used to say to me that before the war he wasn't even allowed to twiddle the knobs on the radio, treated us like big kids. I got a cheque just a year or so ago I shared out between all of us but it wasn't for the same amount they owed him and they say they'll send the rest in instalments. Yeah! I bet! In **stall** ments is the word. Still, I've got Warren's share tucked away for him and those brothers of his never smooth-talked me out of that. They said it was silly, we'd never see him again, but I put my foot down there.

Albert left all these notebooks. I've got them tucked away in that old suitcase somewhere. I'll read them to Warren. That'll be just like sitting on the mat and learning from the old people, learning from Albert. Bub can know all the pride and none of the shame. He doesn't need to know the bad stuff about his father. I've carried them around all these years and read them so much till I know bits by heart. It's like hearing Albert talking again. It's the best of him really. 'Those who seemed to have mastered the English spoke openly in public gatherings using most complicated words right out of Webster or Oxford but were really blind to the fundamental idea of communication. I would label them as linguistic exhibitionists.' 'Linguistic exhibitionists', I always laugh when I read that, that's Albert alright. 'I've been in company with Islanders and Europeans and the Islander has asked me, begged me, not to use his traditional native name and pleaded with me to be introduced as John or Martha or Jack.' Or Albert for that matter. Silly old bugger.

'We were led to believe in a variety of myths which made us subject to the superior culture forced down our throats. There was one myth about classification of people based on a fictional hierarchy.' And Albert used to sing it like those 'do, re, me' scales we learnt at school and do this 'up-the-ladder dance.' Aborigine, Bushman, Hottentot, Kaffir, Zulu, Maori, American Indian, Papuan, Torres Strait Islander, South Sea Islander, European. And then he'd do his 'down-the-ladder dance.' European, South Sea Islander, Torres Strait Islander, Papuan, American Indian, Maori, Zulu, Kaffir, Hottentot, Bushman, Aborigine.

'My interpretation of history is not what happened in the past but how it is told.' He had a real Kuiam's head on his shoulders in those days. But the piss knocks out that mind power eventually, no matter how strong you have it and Albert had it really, really strongly.

'A mighty weapon used to dominate was the introduction of overgenerosity. This custom persists to this day. If there is a disagreement between an Islander and an outsider the Islander usually pleases the other by agreeing on the decision whether he likes it or not. This is considered an act of love which I label artificial ethic imposed to suppress the culture resulting in the development of inferiority complex. This is the beginning of cultural erosion.'

Albert thought of this kind of thing all the time. He'd want me to tell Warren as much as I could. He always sat the kids down on the mat after tea and talked to them. Told them stories. He said we had to keep telling our stories no matter what. Even if they were sad or hard because we were being forced into a sort of amnesia and with the wireless and education all our stories were being lost and our identities as Islanders were going with them and our language and culture and we were trying to make ourselves up in the image of Kole. And he used to say, and more and more as his drinkin days were really on him, he used to say 'Our identity is becoming only a torturing dream' and that's what happened, what he used to yell about in the Horrors. Because he was an initiated man from Mabuiag and knew a lot of useless stuff that he couldn't even pass on to his boys.

'... you've grown him up well my little sick, ruined Bub ... like a monster when I last saw him Mum ... I am so happy that my poor baby found someone to love him and look after him ... I would love to have done that myself ... you're his white Mum but I'm his Black Mum, OK ... yes, I'll call her Mum ... I'll teach you some Islander cooking, Mum ... just rice first though ... you white women can't even cook rice properly—boil it up and stir it—ugh! all mushy and ruined ... and come up and stay with us at Christmas, you're part of the family now ... we'll call you Mum now because you are my son's mother ... I'll make you

my wauri tebud ... if I give you shell you're more than blood
family ... I'll get the boys to send one down here ... it covers
everything that wauri shell ... it's very precious ... it could save
your life ... it could give you plenty of things and make friends
for all time ... you can't forget ... you can't make things wrong
when you have a wauri tebud given to you that way ... your
wauri tebud is just like the boy or girl born from your family ...
it's like adopting him or her ... it's like one part of the Gospel
'Be kind to one another' ... I can growl you if you're my blood
tebud ... have true growl then just finish, no more ... but you
never never growl your wauri tebud because you be ashamed of
yourself ... yes ... I'll make you wauri tebud then I can give you
my boy properly after all these years ... then I can call you Mum
and you can call me Mum.'

She laughed at me when I called her 'Mum'. It hurt a lot
when she did that but, when I thought about it later, I realised
that she probably didn't understand, yet.

And she probably wouldn't understand now. Just think it's
pagan ways, giving shell. She'd probably give me glass beads and
mirrors back. Later maybe. But I can still call her Mum to begin
with and try to explain. Maybe give her shell later on. Yes!

The spirit is there. The spirit is here.

'... wish I could get all togged up and take you down to
the Club, Bub ... put in a few coins ... wait for that winning
line ... you'd bring me luck my Lucky Number 13 ... I can hear
that little winning tune ... hallelujah, hallelujah ... feel those
gold coins pouring into my hands ... cashed up for the Island
... we'll catch that little white plane back into the blue together
my Bub.'

Join the Reef Club. Special Events. Bonus Vouchers. Daily
Draws. Darnley Deeps. Bonus Pearls. Mystery Prizes. Senior

Specials. Birthday Bonus. Tombstone Treasure Troves Precious Beyond Measure.

'... I've cooked you up some pearl-meat sambal, Dad ... I mean Kuiam ... I mean Albert ... I mean Warren ... I mean Mum ... my mouth's watering already.

'... I must have eaten too many of those 'wonky berries' myself Bub ... because I want to go back there now ... to see it again before I die ... it's still a shithole but I want to take you back with me Bub ... you can meet all your relatives, they're all over there.'

That little white plane flew off into the blue with my Bub but now he's coming back. Things are returned.

'... I'll sit you down on the mat after tea Bub ... and all the children and grandchildren too and tell them everything ... all about Albert and Dad and Mum and all the truths about the past ... I'll read out Albert's notebooks and poems and tell them all about Sir and Kevin and Uncle Tommy and Cherbourg ... about Sarita and Koiki Mabo and the war and Phyllis Yamashita ... everything.'

The spirit was there. The spirit is here.

'waiye, e eya e, waiye, e eya eya o
ura bauna a naka gimal o e
zagul maluka eya eya o'

I'm gunna chew that kai-kai tonight.

Afterword

There are sacred scar trees still standing in parks, forests and avenues in cities around this country. From their ancient past people would cut their bark and burl and make canoes and coolamons. Seasons bring new growth but the old scars remain. They reveal a history to be remembered and told.

The characters in this book are the mirror image of us. The book exposes the scars we harbour deep within us; scars we dare not reveal ourselves from fear of shame, guilt and backlash from our society and our community that have shaped our psyche.

We feel a sense of relief that someone as bold as the author has spoken out for us. From the despair of her own experience, she has found a cure—truth, love and compassion for others.

Our scars will heal.

Ricardo Idagi
Murray (Mer) Islander, musician and artist

Acknowledgments

The events portrayed in the novel are also the basis of the script that I wrote for the feature-length film entitled *Call Me Mum*. The film was developed with assistance from SBS Independent, Film Victoria and the Australian Film Commission. It was produced in 2005 by Big and Little Films Pty Ltd for broadcast on SBS Television and directed by Margot Nash. The film was first screened at the 2006 Sydney International Film Festival.

I would like to thank Dimple Bani for his permission to dedicate my novel to Ephraim Bani.

I also thank the Australia Council and Arts Victoria for funding to research and develop the film and the play, *Buyback* on which *Paydirt* is based.

I would like to acknowledge a number of people who have made this book possible: Mabuiag Elder, Ephraim Bani, for our discussions on Islander culture and history over a number of years of rewrites; Aunty Ella Pitt and the women I met and spoke with on my numerous trips to Cairns and Thursday Island; Ricardo Idagi, the Melbourne-based Murray (Mer) Islander, artist and musician for his sensitive reading of the various drafts; my partner Pascale Baelde, a savage editor whose fearless red pen carved swathes from my original verbosity; my friend and editor Angela Rockel for her care and red-penpersonship;

and my friend and colleague Marion M. Campbell for her support and the finesse of her insightful comments. Everyone at UWA Press has been unfailingly helpful and professional and I would especially like to thank the Director, Terri-ann White, for her generous and tireless support of innovative writing, and the editor, Susan Midalia, for her thorough and detailed attention.

The following sources have been used in the writing of this novel:

Ephraim Bani, 'Revelation cultural erosion: Torres Strait situation', pamphlet AIATSIS, 1988. Pages 138 and 159–60 use ideas adapted from this source and in conversation with the author.

Francis Calvert, *Cracks in the Mask*, produced by Lindsey Morrison and Francis Calvert and published by Talking Pictures, Sydney, 1997.

S. J. Earle, 'A Question of Defence: the story of Green Hill Fort, Thursday Island', Torres Strait Historical Society, Thursday Island, 1993.

Ron Edwards, 'Traditional Torres Strait Island Cooking', The Rams Skull Press, Kuranda, 1988.

Ellie Gaffney, *Somebody now: the autobiography of Ellie Gaffney a woman of Torres Strait*, Aboriginal Studies Press for the Australian Institute of Aboriginal Studies, Canberra, 1989.

Elizabeth Osborne, *Torres Strait Islander Women and the Pacific War*, Aboriginal Studies Press, Canberra, 1997. Page 156 uses ideas adapted from this source.

Brian Robinson, 'Ilan Pasin: Torres Strait Art (this is our way)', Exhibition Curator Tom Mosby, Research and development, Brian Robinson, Cairns Regional Gallery, Cairns, 1998. Page 128 uses ideas adapted from this source.

Nonie Sharp, *The Stars of Tagai: The Torres Strait Islanders*, Aboriginal Studies Press, Canberra, 1993. Pages 151 and 157 use ideas adapted from this source.

'Torres Strait at War: a recollection of wartime experiences', Thursday Island State High School, 1987.

I also wish to thank the following people for permission to quote the words of the various songs used in the novel:

'Pinball Wizard'

Words and music by Pete Townshend

© Fabulous Music Pty Ltd adm. by Essex Music Australia Pty Ltd.

All rights reserved. International copyright secured.

Reprinted with permission.

Dimple Bani, for the song 'Awaial', composed by Scotty Misi.

Anne Barby, for the song 'Frangipani Land', composed by Rita Mills, with lyrics by Vicki Saylor.

Lizzie Lui, for the song 'Cakaros', written and composed by Patrick Thaiday.

Judah Toby Senior, for the song 'Waiye', composed by Ganadine Toby.

The song 'Old T. I.' is a traditional song from the Torres Strait which may originally have been a song sung by the Kanakas who were thrown off boats or jumped ship as they were being returned to Vanuatu. If this is the case, then T. I. probably referred to Tanna Island in Vanuatu.

It is acknowledged that the following are registered trademarks: Adora Cream Wafers, Aramis, Armani, Axminster carpets, Biro, Blundies, Brewer's Yeast, Bohemia Crystal, Bon-vita, Bunnykins, Clarke's shoes, Dalton china, Dresden china, Dulux, Encyclopædia Britannica, Enos, Estapol, Eveready, Globite, Hallmark Greeting Cards, Horlicks, Matchbox toys, Mikimoto Pearls, Milo, Miracoil, Nulla-Nulla soap, Paddlepops, Persil, Primate, Ratsak, Sandler, Shelley china, Sportscraft, Steinway, Sustogen, Taubmans, Timezone, Twinings, Twisties, Vegemite, Vicks, Victoria sponge, Vitaglow, Volvo, Wedgwood, Westminster carpets.

If any white foster/adoptive parents, Aborigines or Islanders who have been adopted or fostered, or siblings, would like to contact the author, they should feel free to email her on <kmfallon@unimelb.edu.au>

Also in the New Writing series

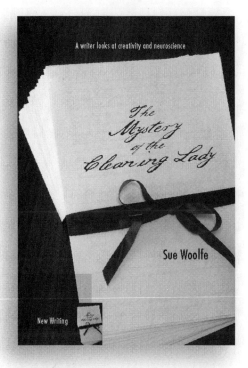

A writer looks at creativity and neuroscience

The Mystery of the Cleaning Lady

Sue Woolfe

New Writing

ISBN 978 1 920694 96 8

Bestselling author Sue Woolfe tracks the journey of her novel, *The Secret Cure*, through her interest in theories about creativity from the field of neuroscience. Continuing the work Woolfe started with Kate Grenville of books *about* writing, this is a fascinating case study of a novel-in-progress.

Praise for The Secret Cure

...this is an outstanding work of imagination, wit and intellect. I await with fascination the future development of this highly talented writer.

Gillian Dooley, *Australian Book Review*

Available now at all good bookstores or order online at www.uwapress.uwa.edu.au

Tel: 08 6488 3670   E-mail: admin@uwapress.uwa.edu.au

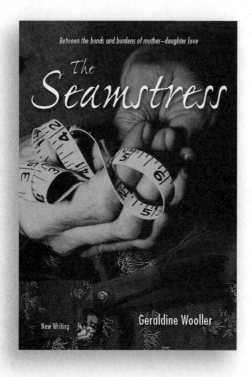

Between the bonds and burdens of mother–daughter love

The Seamstress

New Writing   Geraldine Wooller

ISBN 978 1 920694 93 7

Jo narrates the story of her strong, passionate mother Willa, whose gradual slide into dementia shifts them into a new and difficult relationship. *The Seamstress* is a memorable tale of friendship and love between women.

> *...a confident, at times even beautiful, narrative weaving time-honoured themes between mothers and daughters, life's tantalising, frustrating search for love and the cruelty of time...*
>
> The Sunday Times

Available now at all good bookstores or order online at www.uwapress.uwa.edu.au

Tel: 08 6488 3670   E-mail: admin@uwapress.uwa.edu.au